What People are Saying

I love funny books, funny movies and funny people. I can't remember when I laughed this hard.

> Debbie Goldstein, Boca Raton, FL

I picked this book out for my Temple Book Club, and it was a HUGE hit!

> Mary Schwartz, Queens, NY

I'm not Jewish and I thought it was hysterical.

> Vinny Castellano, West Caldwell, NJ

Men, women, Jews and non-Jews will flash back to their own hilarious misadventures.

> Sharon Klapowitz, Chicago, IL

I got this book as a gift, and I thank my friend over and over again.

> Tom Jenkins, San Francisco, CA

Reading this book was like hanging out with your funniest friend!

> Sara Cohen, Miami, FL

Why Jews Don't Camp

*Plus 24 Other Hilarious Stories
About Everyday Life*

By Arnie Z. Goldberg

Laugh Out Loud Publishing
Boca Raton, Florida

Published by

Laugh Out Loud Publishing

21218 St. Andrews Blvd.

#227

Boca Raton, FL 33433

www.LOLpub.com

1st Edition Copyright 2007 by Arnie Z. Goldberg

Library of Congress Catalog Number 2007922990

ISBN-13: 978-0-9793278-0-3

ISBN-10: 0-9793278-0-6

Printed by RJ Communications LLC NY

Printed in the United States of America

Contents

Dedication

This is probably the only comedy book that begins with a story about a hospice. In fact, I am certain that if I ever took a professional writing class they would recommend strongly against it. But since I rarely follow what I'm told to do, I can't see starting now.

I am dedicating this book to my Dad, Bernie, who passed away in a Palm Beach County hospice a few years ago at the age of 85. I'm not sure if having a sense of humor is genetic or environmental but I was brought up listening to some of the best and worst jokes ever, and he clearly was involved with some of my genes—my mother swears to it.

I mention the hospice because on the day before he passed away I visited with him and we had this heart-to-heart talk about life and death. He was not in pain and he was at peace with his next stop. He had some drugs in his system that made him quite tired, and as he fell asleep I began to leave the room for probably the last time. As I got to the door, I heard a pleading voice say "Arnie, Arnie, come back, I have something to tell you." I rushed back, surprised how insistent his voice sounded. Thinking this was one of the most important, perhaps last thing he might tell me, I leaned in close. This was the conversation that followed:

Dad: "Hot."

Me: "Do you want me to turn up the air-conditioning?"

Dad: "No, it's hot in Florida."

Me: "I know."

Dad: "Easy to get chapped lips."

Me: "O.K., what about chapped lips?"

Dad: "Do you know the best way to prevent chapped lips?"

Me: "With that lip balm stuff?" (I was totally befuddled by this point.)

Dad: "No — camel poop."

Me: Convinced that the drugs had taken over my Dad's brain and trying to be nice, I asked: "Does camel poop have special ingredients in it?"

Dad: "No, but it'll keep you from doing this..." Then he slowly (on purpose) licked his lips from one end to the other. He winked at me, smiled widely, closed his eyes, and went to sleep.

From the beginning to quite literally the end, he was always telling jokes. Thanks, Dad!

Acknowledgements

Before I started this book, I had no idea I was going to write a book. Sitting in a lantern-lit tent at 5:00 a.m., camping out for the very first time, I was having a miserable experience. Miserable to me, but quite funny to others as it turned out. Since I had nothing but time in those wee hours, I started writing down on scraps of paper how insane things had gotten over the last 24 hours. I later typed up the story in my mosquito-free house (fully covered in calamine lotion), and shared it with some friends who laughed out loud. They shared it with some more friends, and pretty soon people were asking if I had any more funny stories I could send them.

So my first acknowledgement has to go to those people who dragged me camping in the first place, and for laughing as they read about my first experience. Thanks Rob, Hector, Sherv, Marty, Jeff, Bill, Mark, Bob, Charlie, Chris D, Gary and Chris P.—the guys from the YMCA Adventure Guides group.

These stories would not be possible without a great set of friends who more often than not got to experience some of these things (although some other things may be best left in our memories).

To the Camp Laff-A-Lot crew (my best friends from college): thanks for making me laugh constantly and giving me plenty of material to work with. Denis & Renee, Tom & Barb, Doug & Mona, Joe & Sherri, Doug & Harriet, Scott & Michelle, Bobby & Amy, Ron & Pia, and Kevin.

To my buddies from Japan where laughing was essential to survival: Amy & Brian, Kim, Emmett & Roni, Dick & Audrey, Blair & Valerie, Carmine, Greg N., Jay, Greg B.—and to Ken who helped me get into and out of the most bizarre situations.

To other friends who gave me great feedback along the way as I wrote the book: Darcy, Cece & Bill, Maureen & Marty, Jeff & Lena, Marcie & Marty, Brooke & Nathan, Lisa & Jeff, Monique, Sarah and Tracey.

And to other great people who have been there in my life and who love to laugh: Carol & Tony, Terry & Kym, Geoff & Mary, Mark M., Felix & Annie, Claude & Hee-Jin, Mike G., Jeff H., Franco, MVB, Nancy, and Calvin & Merceles.

Without my family none of this would have been possible. My Mom & Dad, my wife Karen, and my sons, Sam & Michael, my brother Allan, his wife Lisa, and their three girls—Kayla, Megan and Amanda, my in-laws Joan & Allen, my brother-in-law Norman, and his family Chris, Ryan, Nyles and Christopher.

I also really need to thank those who took my thoughts, scribbles and ramblings and made them into a real live book.

To Jeannie, my editor (Claire Communications, Inc.)—
thanks for turning my sentences and paragraphs into English.
I guess I really did earn that C in English grammar in 12th
grade.

To Kim, my illustrator (www.bolithoart.com) and great
friend from our days in Japan—thank you for your brilliant
illustrations and for capturing the funny moments with a great
edginess.

To Rick, my book cover designer (Synthesis Design)—
Awesome job! I remember being in the bookstore with you
looking at different books and their covers. You said you
would make a cover that would really stand out and you
delivered!

To Ron, my printer, (www.BooksJustBooks.com) and book
consultant—while there are a whole host of companies that
can print books, there is no printing company like yours that
goes that extra step, every time to make an author feel like
the best product is going to come out at the end.

To Steve, my publisher (Laugh Out Loud Publishing www.
LOLpub.com), thanks for taking a chance on this first-time
author. Without you, this book would not have gotten into
anyone's hands. We have a lot in common, so good luck with
your mission of producing great books and articles that make
people laugh.

Foreword

I have never been quite sure whether I seek out weird, funny situations or whether they just seem to find me. I decided to write this book because I had shared many of these stories with friends and strangers alike, and they always laughed out loud and often could very much relate to the stories.

Enjoy the book. I'm sure you'll see yourself or one of your friends or family members in these stories!

Check us out at www.whyjewsdontcamp.com or www.arnieZgoldberg.com

- Email some of my favorite chapters for free to your friends and family;
- Find a free collection of great jokes that you can help add to;
- Add your name to our email list;
- Learn more about things we are doing!

Send an email to arnie@whyjewsdontcamp.com to let me know what you think of the book. I promise to respond!

Whether you're lying on a couch or standing in a bookstore, whether you're a book reviewer, a potential distributor, or just an average guy (or gal) looking for a laugh, I really do appreciate your help in making this book successful. I'm hoping you will laugh out loud today, tomorrow, and every day!

I. Oy Vey!

I'M JEWISH, I AM the least handy person I know, I'm a hypochondriac, I whine (only on occasion, I think), and I have always been adverse to contact sports except for watching them on television. Sound familiar?

I was born in Queens, grew up on Long Island, and now live in Boca Raton, Florida. My hometown on Long Island, which was 90% Jewish, has the distinction of being the only town where Home Depot ever went out of business, as there turned out to be so few do-it-yourself Jews. A big surprise? I think not.

A Jewish Scavenger Hunt

My father-in-law, who is not an expert on Jewish customs and who thinks I'm a bit nuts anyway, just shook his head in amazement when he saw me stumbling down the street to his waiting car with this long robe on and my beltless pants down around my knees.

The fall season is a wonderful time of year. The leaves start changing color up north, baseball season has its playoffs, football season is underway, and the temperature starts cooling off (from 90 degrees to 88 degrees in South Florida). It also begins the annual Jewish scavenger hunt that many people are not aware of. It is the exciting search for *free* High Holy Day tickets.

As background for non-Jews who may not know, Rosh Hashanah and Yom Kippur are the most important of all Jewish Holidays. Rosh Hashanah, the Jewish New Year, is a time for family gatherings and sweet-tasting foods. Yom Kippur, the Day of Atonement, is the most solemn day and is a day of fasting and praying.

From my experience there are four types of Jewish people:

1) Those who belong year-round to a local temple and pay annual dues;
2) Those who buy tickets to a local temple for just the High Holy Days (usually $150-$200 per person);
3) Those who never attend temple; and
4) Those (perhaps only my brother and me) who are either so cheap or just enjoy the sport of trying to find **free** tickets.

Obviously, the "real" temples that sell tickets also don't give away free tickets even though some claim they don't turn anyone away. What that really means is that if you have the $200, they'll take you even if you didn't buy the tickets in advance.

When I was young, my family fell into the first category. My brother and I had a bar mitzvah and regularly attended synagogue. The "real" temples are beautiful, with first-class rabbis and great-singing cantors where everyone looks their Saturday-best.

As I got older and left the confines of my parents, I developed all kinds of new habits, most of them bad (but they were plenty of fun). As a single person and someone who moved quite a bit as my jobs changed, I didn't join a temple. As the High Holy Day season rolled around, I would see the big newspaper ads for "non-affiliated" people:

"Nomadic-Jews, Come and celebrate the High Holy Days with Temple Beth-Shlomo" or

"Got $200? Come pray with us at "Temple We Are The Chosen Ones."

Not having a lot of money and thinking that was a pretty big chunk to pay for a few hours of praying, my brother and I decided to see if there was any way around shelling out so much money.

We searched the newspaper for better deals but couldn't find any in the standard sections of the paper. It was relatively expensive to advertise in the newspaper so we almost gave up. Luckily one of us was looking in the personal ads under "Women Seeking Women" (probably just an honest mistake, but not a bad one) and actually saw a tiny ad for "New Jewish Temple forming, FREE Tickets."

We literally jumped for joy, first because we would be going for free, and second, that we found some very interesting requests in the personals section we had stumbled onto.

We called the phone number and they gave us an address to go to the following day for the first night of Rosh Hashanah. We got dressed in our suits, had our yarmulkes, and were so excited that we had an extra $200 in our wallets.

As we got closer to the address, we were stunned to see only one building within a mile of the location. It was the town's bowling center. Believing that we wrote the address down incorrectly, we started driving away when we noticed a group of others with their yarmulkes on heading toward the bowling alley. There was also a large group of Italian men with gold chains and bowling shirts that said "Vinny's Pizzeria" going in as well. We were frozen in indecision, but somehow our legs moved to enter. It turns out that the rabbi who was forming the new temple had rented a large room in the bowling alley (usually where children's birthday parties are held) to save on costs. (I guess when everyone is going for free it's hard to expect a comparable Temple Beth-Shlomo design, but a freakin' bowling alley?)

About 20 people showed up (some appeared to be Jewish lesbians given the placement of the newspaper ad), all a bit astonished as to the location but realizing that we pretty much deserved this since we were trying to beat the system.

As we began, the bowling alley was not particularly crowded so the noise wasn't too bad. However, as the religious service moved along it became increasingly louder. When the rabbi told us to take a moment of silence for deep reflection, and the Pizzeria Boys started screaming about making three strikes in a row, it kind of ruined the moment. We made it through the two-hour ceremony a bit embarrassed that we had sunk that low. The only good news was that the bowling alley gave us free bowling shoes for that night after the service was over. My brother and I had never prayed and bowled in the same night before, so that was at least novel. We did lose to one lesbian couple who were quite good bowlers.

The next year I was married to a non-Jew (more on that story later) so I was still on my own with my brother. We pledged we'd never be so desperate again, but the lure and excitement of the hunt for free tickets was like an adrenaline rush. But we did agree we'd never do the bowling alley again.

Again our search for newspaper ads in the standard section of the paper proved fruitless for free tickets. We checked the Women Seeking Women section again (we actually did this daily for the whole year in case there were early mentions of free tickets) but there was nothing.

My brother got a Singles magazine in the mail and in it was our Nirvana — free High Holy Day tickets, as they were trying to make sure that Jews married each other and they felt the lure of free tickets would get lots of singles there. Being married, I felt very torn. Should I lie about being single on the most religious days when God was deciding my fate for the next year, or save $200? Plus I was worried my wife wouldn't be all too happy with me attending a singles event. I chose saving the money and hoped God would understand that as a good Jew I was always looking to save a buck and that my wife would realize I was simply out of my mind (which she already knew).

We showed up at a nicer place than the bowling alley (pretty low benchmark to beat) but at a place not quite as nice as "Temple We Are The Chosen Ones." I kept my left hand in my pants pocket as we entered, as my wedding ring would have barred me from entrance. Even inside I was very careful about this, and looked quite bizarre trying to hold and turn the pages of the prayer book with just my right hand.

What I thought was going to be a serious religious experience turned more into a speed dating event as the rabbi made all the men take turns meeting all the women individually for the first 30 minutes hoping that sparks would fly. The women I met all seemed a bit concerned that I had my left hand in my pants pocket for so long and wondered what my hand was doing there. Given that many of the men were old and fat (I was still years away from reaching that peaceful place), I didn't seem too bad to them, so I was the target of three or four of the women. I was actually called up to the pulpit to select one of the women to worship next to for the service.

I thought of my wife and the embarrassment this would cause her, but selected Shirley Finklestein, as I didn't want to blow my cover and, most importantly, my free admission. The service was nice, and Shirley helped me turn the pages in my book (I told her I had a skin disease on my left hand that was healing after my trip down the Amazon River. She was very impressed as she didn't know Jews did such adventurous things). The service ended and it was nice to see that some of the people looked like they had paired up quite nicely. I told Shirley that while it was nice to meet her, I was moving to Israel next week and that I needed to go now to catch up with some year-ago friends at a bowling party—I hoped I would still get the free shoes. She was saddened, but thrilled to hear that I was going to work on a kibbutz in Israel and help poor people. I got home to my wife and decided that I was never, ever going this free ticket route again.

The following year, my wife and I decided to go to Tampa during the High Holy Days to visit my Episcopalian in-laws, which was fine with me as I had enough of the Boca Raton scavenger hunt for free tickets.

My in-laws knew about my passion for free tickets and somehow my mother-in-law was able to find me one ticket to a temple a couple of miles from where they lived. I didn't ask any questions as I was thrilled that I could attend services (I had a lot of confessing to do that year) for free again. I guess my never, ever resolution didn't last too long.

My father-in-law drove me down to the temple, which was quite beautiful on the outside. No bowling alley, no warehouse loft. I was thrilled. I walked in and was immediately taken aback by the incredible amount of hugging going on between members. People were not dressed in suits or dresses, but long, cottony robes. I got to the registration table and was welcomed by a hug. I explained to them that I was visiting from Boca Raton so they summoned the head of New Guest Registrations, who gave me a big hug of course. He told me to take off my suit jacket, my tie and my belt and store them in an open, nearby locker. I had no idea what was going on. He told me that their members pray comfortably and he handed me a long robe, which I dutifully put on.

I made it to my seat, managing to avoid some of the hugs (one woman almost fell down as she got stuck in mid-lunge when I head-faked right and went left quickly to avoid her—like a Jewish Barry Sanders for those 10 seconds), but still got caught in the grasp of a few. I opened the prayer book and saw that it belonged to the Messianic Temple of Tampa. Not really knowing what Messianic meant, I read on:

"Messianic Judaism is a Biblically-based movement of people who, as committed Jews, believe in Jesus as the Jewish Messiah of Israel."

Wow, was I in the wrong place. I yearned for the noise of the bowling alley and the adoration of Shirley Finklestein. They sat me in the middle of their congregation so there was no way out. It was strange watching people pray to Jesus wearing a yarmulke during Rosh Hashanah. I got really nervous when Sister Jonah and Brother Elijah told me they were serving Kool-Aid in the back of the room after the service. I had an instantaneous flashback of the Jim Jones/Guyana cult and their Kool-Aid drinking which got me twitching in my robe. The service ended after two long hours. I have never held hands, chanted and swayed so much in my life. I was able to sneak out the side door in my robe (I left my suit coat, tie and belt there). My father-in-law, who is not an expert on Jewish customs and who thinks I'm a bit nuts anyway, just shook his head in amazement when he saw me stumbling down the street to his waiting car with this long robe on and my beltless pants down around my knees. I think for a moment (or perhaps longer) he wondered what his only daughter had gotten herself into or how she might get herself out of the situation.

When I got back to their house, my wife looked at me a bit astonished, and as I tried to explain the story it got more and more impossible to get the words out. My mother-in-law, who is the sweetest person in the whole world, said, "I hope everything worked out well, and I really like that robe on you."

I am back in Boca now 2 days from Rosh Hashanah and have put aside the $200 to buy my first High Holy Day ticket. I'm planning on buying the ticket today, but man that new video iPod model certainly looks cool to buy instead. I'm just going to take one quick glance at the newspaper to see if there are any free ticket deals...

Why Jews Don't Camp

I peered out from a small tent flap and saw it was a band of hyperactive, potentially rabies-carrying raccoons high on Krispy Kremes and seeking out a midnight snack.

Growing up in Queens there weren't a whole lot of opportunities or places to set up a tent (too much concrete), roast marshmallows by a campfire (too many fires related to arson already), or watch the stars (too much air pollution to see them). Plus camping isn't particularly easy (bugs, heat, rain, and hard ground) so only the tougher kids in my neighborhood (Vinny, Nunzio, and Julio) could deal with it on those rare occasions when there was a camping trip out of the City. My best friends Irving and Morty and I weren't considered particularly tough—in fact when the word "weenies" was mentioned around us it wasn't referring to the little hot dogs.

Years later, married with kids in Boca Raton, I was looking for a father-son bonding program. I joined the *Adventure Guides* group with about a hundred other Dads and their sons divided into 10 groups. This program is organized by the local YM<u>C</u>A, not the YM<u>J</u>A (Young Men's <u>Jewish</u> Association), which is an important point. It turns out that non-Jews like to camp, know how to camp and actually own tents. The few Jews in the group like to stay in fancy hotels or attend only safe indoor events like bowling.

My eight-year-old son Michael had been asking me for years when he would have the opportunity like his Italian/WASP friends to actually go on a camping trip. I'd been good at avoiding this, or bribing him to forget about it, but it finally became impossible to ignore the "beautiful Jonathan Dickenson State Park Camping Trip excursion," which was only one day and one night. We signed up along with six other Dads from our small group and 30-40 other dads from the entire Boca YMCA. How bad could 24 hours be?????

9:00 a.m.

We began our day at the local supermarket buying the key supplies: three giant bags of Doritos, two giant bags of marshmallows, a box of donuts, and a case of beer. The girl at the cash register commented that it was one of the more interesting combinations she had rung up in awhile. When I got home, my wife sent me back to the store to buy hamburgers, buns, bottled water, ice, ketchup, cereal bars, napkins, plastic utensils, garbage bags, suntan lotion, and bug spray. I chose a different girl at the register to ring me up. I didn't see any of my Christian group members at the store, as they seemed to be much more organized with their detailed checklists and had bought the key items in advance. I did see the one other Jewish guy from one of the other YMCA groups with basically the same items as I had purchased in my first go-around. His wife was out of town, so hopefully he and his child would survive the trip.

10:00 a.m. – 1:00 p.m.

I spent the next few hours packing clothes and other items and resting a lot, as I knew the next 22 hours could be some of the hardest of my life. I had a small bag with one extra shirt for Michael and me, a sleeping bag, and a tent borrowed from a neighbor. My wife got a much bigger suitcase out and packed extra underwear, socks, shorts, more shirts, toothbrushes, flashlights, an air mattress, pillows and a radio. I felt bad that I couldn't find the wife-less person from the supermarket who I'm sure only had a "small" bag like my first attempt.

1:00 p.m. – 3:00 p.m.

We packed up the car and headed north for the hour-plus drive to the "scenic" campground. We arrived at the Ranger station and were told that we had site #114, one of their best. Michael and I were excited. We drove and drove and finally got to our plot of land. It was "nestled" next to hundreds of other plots that looked remarkably similar to the plot in my backyard, making me wonder why we had to drive almost 90 minutes in the first place.

3:00 p.m.- 5:00 p.m.

I unpacked the car and got set for the critical job of setting up the borrowed tent. Having absolutely no idea what to do with the paper-thin plastic thing and lots of long poles, I looked at the instructional manual. The tent was made in China, and the instructions appeared to be in the same language. Frustrated, I walked around and happened to come across the whimpering, Jewish, wife-less guy from the supermarket who somehow managed to have his tent practically upside down, which made me feel better.

I was determined to figure it out. I looked carefully at all sides of the tent and concluded, "No problem, let me pay someone who knows what to do." Fifteen minutes later, albeit with a lighter wallet, my tent looked fabulous. It even had that canopy thing on top in case it rained. I told the crew constructing my tent that it wasn't necessary as the weatherman said there was zero chance of rain that night, but they said, "from our experience you never trust the weatherman." I chuckled under my breath at their extreme caution and told them that the guy from the supermarket with the upside down tent didn't think it was necessary either. It was an absolutely beautiful day without a cloud in the sky.

As I went to unpack the car, I discovered some good news and some bad news. The bags with the Doritos, marshmallows, beer and donuts arrived safely, but in my excitement I had somehow left behind the cooler with my kid's water and his food for dinner and breakfast. I tried to talk him into surviving on just Doritos, donuts and marshmallows but even he wasn't buying. So instead of a nice afternoon canoeing, some of the Dads and I went off to the supermarket to buy the things left behind. While we were gone, my tent was used as a play area for the kids, so the amount of sand inside the sleeping bags, on top of the air mattress, and touching the pillows may have broken some camping records.

5:00 p.m. - 7:30 p.m.

We arrived back at the campground and made a great campfire. I tried to help but wound up spilling lots of lighter fluid on my pants and socks, so I backed away from the fire as I didn't want to be the kindling. I decided to sit in a chair and drink beer with a few of the other Dads. After about four beers, I felt like a great camper and barely noticed all the kids throwing leaves, rocks, bottles, cups, shirts and sneakers into the fiercely raging fire. In fact, I was surprised later when my son's eyebrows actually appeared singed.

One of the Dads, Marty, took charge and did a great job cooking up the hot dogs and burgers. I drank more beer and started to see how many giant bags of Doritos could really be consumed in a two-hour period. I think I surprised a lot of people by my dedication and success.

After dinner the kids toasted marshmallows and everyone was happy. One of the Dads handed out wooden sticks for this, but I cleverly gave mine a metal one as I thought the wooden one would burn. As I was downing my seventh beer (I wanted to make sure I would sleep through the night), I heard a very loud scream and saw a kid running to me (turned out to be mine). Who can always remember things like metal being such a great conductor of heat? The hand he had been using to hold the metal rod for the marshmallows was burning up. Guess it wasn't a clever idea after all. We applied some ice and the blisters seemed to not be so bad an hour later.

7:30 p.m. – 9:00 p.m.

One of the morally upstanding YMCA Dads had gotten his hands on a pirated DVD of *The Incredibles* and set up a viewing for the 100 YMCA attendees on a giant white screen in the main park area. It was an absolutely beautiful night as the stars were out and there wasn't a cloud in the sky. While the picture quality was only fair and the audio was tough to hear, what better way to spend an evening than watching a pirated DVD of a movie you had paid $10 to see in the movie theater only a few days before?

When the movie was halfway done, Michael and I headed back to our tent to go to sleep, pleased about our successful day (his blisters had really subsided by then) of camping.

9:00 p.m. - midnight

We arrived back at our campsite and noticed that the box of six chocolate donuts left on the picnic table was pulverized and not a trace of a donut existed. Turns out a hungry raccoon or two had wandered in for dessert. We got in our two-man tent and were really pleased with how well our father-son outing was going. We zipped up all the sides of our tent, except for the very bottom part that I didn't know about. As we got in our sleeping bags and tried to push away the piles of irritating sand inside, we noticed the unbelievably loud noise coming from a nearby cricket convention. For the next two hours, it sounded like they were actually inside our brains. The only thing that kept the cricket noise from totally blowing us away was the even louder music and drunken conversation coming from our neighbor's campsite. Somehow Michael fell asleep. About midnight the noise died down.

Midnight – 2:00 a.m.

Finally some peace and quiet and the beer buzz was starting to fade, so I was ready for bed. As I was almost asleep I heard some footsteps and scratching on the tent. I thought it was a guy in our group so I whispered all the possible names. I heard no reply, just more and more scratching. I peered out from a small tent flap and saw it was a band of hyperactive, potentially rabies-carrying raccoons high on Krispy Kremes and seeking out a midnight snack. Not only was this freaking me out, but all that beer consumed throughout the day was beginning to need a release. I felt like I was in an episode of *Fear Factor*. Can you relieve yourself without being attacked by a group of crazy, hyped-up raccoons waiting to tear down your tent? I started to undo the zipper at the front of the tent, but when I heard increased footsteps and hissing I backed off quickly. I tried to think like a non-Jew, but I kept on drawing a blank. I promised never to drink again if I could get out of this situation safely. The desire to go to the bathroom was reaching epidemic levels at the same time that the raccoons seemed to call in additional reinforcements. I was stuck with the potential of relieving myself inside the tent which I just couldn't do. Somehow I came up with the idea of lying down sideways and aiming through an opening with the tent zipper just a little bit "exposed". I can't begin to describe how hard this was to do, or how close the tent zipper and pants zipper came to "capturing me," but I was able to get past the brutal problem. I believe the raccoons were in complete awe!

2:00 a.m. – 5:00 a.m.

I was finally ready for bed. Absolutely exhausted, I was thinking about how brilliant I had been never to camp before. It started as a small patter on top of the tent and I chuckled that this little rain had come but was soon to end. At almost the exact moment the smile appeared on my face, the rain intensified and the tent got pelted. The weatherman's forecast was only off by 100%! Water began to seep in and then pour in along with all kinds of buzzing mosquitoes that must have heard from the crickets or raccoons that that there was a newbie Jewish guy invading their land. I was attacked and felt it. Michael was still asleep and only realized he had welts from the mosquitoes when he woke in the morning. My clothes were wet, my sleeping bag was wet, my pillow was drenched and I still didn't even understand where the water was coming from. Who knew that the zipper at the bottom of the tent was so critical?

5:00 a.m. – 7:00 a.m.

Michael awoke to the ending rain, in a puddle of water, scratching everywhere. He ignored me when I asked if he had enjoyed camping out. We got out of the tent and saw everything we had left outside (too buzzed and lazy to put it away the night before) completely soaked. We did manage to find some chocolate chip cookies and donuts at a friend's campsite, and plowed through them like they were lobster dripping with butter. We threw all of our wet stuff into the car and headed home. We thought we were smart to leave our only pair of sneakers outside the tent before we went to bed, but certainly learned how tough it is to drive a car with all that squishing going on. We did manage to catch a glimpse of the Jewish guy who I saw in the supermarket at his campsite crying hysterically with his son yelling at him.

8:30 a.m.

We arrived home exhausted, bitten up, and bewildered. As I crawled into bed I couldn't help notice the new flyer that arrived yesterday from the YMCA pronouncing that it was time to sign up for the next Camping Extravaganza happening in three weeks. I slowly ripped it to shreds.

I called Morty and Irving when I woke up several hours later and promised I would stick to bowling-only events and become an *Adventure Guide* "Indoorsman."

Are Jews Thrifty or Cheap?

Eating out with other couples can wreak havoc on the tradeoff between a Jew's manhood and a Jew's tight wallet—the one that's hard to reach when you keep your arms firmly attached to your sides as people are waiting for you to reach for it.

Many people think Jewish people are cheap. I prefer to think of Jews as "thrifty." Here are two stories for you to think about.

When I was a young kid I used to get my hair cut at a neighborhood place for about $6, which was fine until my Mom read about a "bargain" in the local *Pennysaver* newspaper.

Mom is the kind of person who was always looking for the best deal. Dragging my Dad along, she would drive for an hour and spend a bunch of money on tolls and gas just to save a few dollars on some basic item. In fact, she would save less than they spent on the driving, but would brag about the savings for a week.

Against that backdrop, my Mom gathered up my brother

and me one Saturday afternoon to start our journey to get our haircut from a new place. Through neighboring towns, onto major highways, and past buildings I had never seen before, we traveled with a defiant purpose, almost mantra—"we're Jewish, and we're going to save some money today." We were in the car for so long that I wondered if we would be going to a place with a different time zone or a different climate.

Finally, Mom stopped the car in this giant parking lot and said, "Get out and hurry, the special is over in 20 minutes," so I realized we had reached our destination.

I looked around and saw that we were at a place called the "Farmer's Market." As we walked into this large one-floor building, I could see that people were selling every kind of fruit and vegetable imaginable. There were also some tsotchke vendors who sold things like Rubik cubes, model cars with glue that smelled really, really good, and special paper airplanes that could only be made to fly by the guy at the booth.

My mom bought food at Waldbaums in cans and packages— I couldn't imagine her buying anything she would put in her mouth or her family's mouth from this flea market array of stalls. We ran past people selling strawberries, lettuce, oranges, broccoli and watermelon, probably much to the surprise of people who all seemed to be strolling as if they were walking through a field (this just happened to be a field of concrete). Our family was not going to miss the "special." My younger brother was getting pulled so hard by my mother that he was virtually airborne.

In the back row, past hundreds of stalls, squished

between the dried cheese vendor (quite the smell in a non-air-conditioned building in August) and the pickle guy, was a small sign that read "HAIRKUTS." I assumed the sign was supposed to say "HAIRCUTS" and that it was not some kind of exotic food I had never heard of.

We walked into the empty stall and sat down. My Mom was amazed that no one else had discovered this "oasis" as she called it. For only $2.50, we could get our haircut or hairkut. I went first and the man (I have trouble calling him a barber) with very shaky hands asked what size I was going to use. I had no idea what he was talking about. Sneering at me like this was my first time at his lovely establishment, he took out three different-sized bowls. I was still confused (and out of breath from running) and couldn't figure out what I would be eating during the haircut. He could tell I was confused, so he took turns plopping each one of the bowls on my head like a hat. Still not quite sure what was going on, my Mom stepped in and chose the two-person salad bowl as my head ornament.

With the bowl firmly on my head, the "hairkut" guy revved up his electric shears (I believe this guy must be living in New Zealand now tending to sheep) and proceeded to shave off every strand of hair not covered by the bowl. On the positive side, the operation only lasted about one minute. On the negative side, I had to leave the stall and go out into the public throngs in the Farmer's Market and later that day to a birthday party.

I still tremble at the memories of those days. The father of one of my best friends seemed less concerned about my ridiculously bad hair or the fact that the kids in the neighborhood called me "Bowl Boy," but regularly asked my Dad if he was concerned that his two boys seemed to smell of cheese.

Eating out with other couples can wreak havoc on the tradeoff between a Jew's manhood and a Jew's tight wallet— the one that's hard to reach when you keep your arms firmly attached to your sides as people are waiting for you to reach for it. After I got married, I would often run into some strange situations going out to eat with a bunch of couples, and I couldn't help but notice that the results would be so different if I only went out with Jewish friends or a combination of Jewish and non-Jewish.

I have found that there are typically three types of ordering behavior for couples, which has caused some major issues when the bill comes:

1) "We don't want an appetizer, but maybe we'll have one basic cocktail, the low-priced entrée, and no dessert."

2) "We definitely want an appetizer, we're going to order two or three name-brand drinks, the moderately-priced entrée, a cappuccino and some dessert."

3) "We want the most expensive appetizers, a couple of bottles of $200 wine, the sparkling water from the artesian in Italy, the largest steak you've got, desserts for the whole table, and some cognac after dinner."

I have found that more often than not when I go out with just Jewish couples, there seems to be high numbers of #1's, and there's never a problem since the bill is simply split evenly among the number of couples.

When I go out with a group of Jews and non-Jews, the trouble begins and all the Jews know it before they even head out.

The first big decision for a Jewish couple when asked to go out is, "Who is going?" You would think it might be, "Where are you going?" or "When are you going?" But the "who" actually dominates the thought process. Some people think it's logical because you want to make sure you're going to have a good time—the reality is they want to know if they have to bring a bagged lunch to work for a week or two instead of eating lunch out.

Let's assume you get the Jews to actually say yes. You arrive at the restaurant and the non-Jews order the beef carpaccio and the salmon special almost before they are seated. Drink orders start flying and they ask for not one, but two wine guys to come over to the table. Main course orders are taken, and lamb chops from lambs in America are not good enough so the New Zealand ones are ordered.

As a Jew, you are faced with some major dilemmas. Do you sit back and watch other couples devour expensive appetizers while you are sipping on your tap water while your stomach growls? Do you decide to order double-shot cocktails with the resultant hangover just to keep up? Instead of ordering the Pasta Primavera since you like to order the lowest-priced dinner and to eat vegetarian late at night, do you order the special super-large Veal Chop that the non-New Zealand lamb chop people are ordering? Do you order the cheesecake even though you are lactose-intolerant?

Let's say there are two Jewish couples and two non-Jewish

couples eating out. The two Jewish couples' bill is $50 for each
couple since they ordered what they normally would (they
are hardcore #1's as categorized above). At the same time, the
non-Jews couples who are having a grand old time, wind up
with a bill that's about $150 per couple. The non-Jews are full,
drunk, and really happy, and haven't been paying attention
to what the Jews are ordering except for the fact that they
seem to be eating more than a normal person's share of the
free bread.

The bill for the eight people comes, and the guy drinking
the cognac does the math and concludes that each couple
needs to put in $100. The people who have been eating and
drinking like kings and queens remark how the bill is less
than normal, while the two Jewish couples who have split
one dessert among the four of them are not sure what to say
or do about the bill that is twice as high than they actually
should be paying.

I've seen Jewish guys "man-up" and just split the bill—not
sure if they should have ordered more or glad they didn't
as the total bill would have been even higher. I've seen the
Jewish guys try to "man-up" before the kicks to their shins
from their wives gets them asking if they think it's fair. This is
usually followed by looks of amazement. I've seen the Jewish
guy say he's only got $50 and that his credit card is at home.
I see this dance so often at the end of a meal it's fascinating
to watch.

I did come up with one strategy that has seemed to work.
I invited my non-Jewish friends to a new Jewish deli (the
one with no liquor license) for knishes, blintzes and gefilte

fish. They were coincidentally busy for that night. It was also unfortunate as they could have seen my new haircut. I just came back from one of those haircut chains where everyone comes out looking the same, and that's the men and women. I only spent $10 (what a bargain) so I've got extra money. Maybe I'll splurge and get one of those large black and white cookies after dinner.

Jewish Men
Who Whine—All?

They even refer to it as "Organ Recital" time (which is not when someone plays a piano) when people sit around a circle at the community pool, pick an organ (heart, lung, liver) and go through the diseases they have had associated with that organ, their friends have had with that organ, and information they have about diseases with that organ.

Almost every Jewish guy I know (and a lot of Jewish women for that matter) whines like a little boy when they are sick. Our "fever" of 98.7 degrees quickly turns into complaining that "this is the hottest I've ever been—it feels like 104 degrees, check the thermometer again." A sniffle turns into "I know I'm coming down with the flu" and guzzling of NyQuil. And maybe even worse, every Jewish guy I know is a hypochondriac.

I was in the dentist's office the other day and my hygienist was telling me about her brother's medical woes. With half her hand in my mouth and the rest of my mouth filled with instruments and gushing water, my attempts to beg her to shut up went for naught. I almost hoped the dentist would start drilling to drown out her rambling. I finished up with the dentist and immediately made three appointments with three different specialists, as I realized I had been experiencing some of the things the hygienist had mentioned!

One of the worst things about having to go to so many different types of doctors so often to check out the non-existent problems, is that you run into a whole bunch of people in waiting rooms that either have real problems or fellow hypochondriacs who think they have real problems. This either confirms that you do have the dreaded condition you came to be checked for, or in the worse case scenario, now may have several additional related problems, as people in waiting rooms can be pretty creative. In Florida, many of them are elderly and have had years to perfect their disease conversation. Many of the doctors' offices (I think it's a marketing ploy to get repeat customers) play into this world of hypochondriacs. I can't remember the exact titles of the magazines in the waiting room but they seemed like they were called *Pancreatic Killers Monthly* and *Fatal Bacterial Infections Digest.* What ever happened to *Highlights?*

It doesn't help that there's a website (www.rarediseases. org) that covers 1,100 rare diseases! I started specifying some of the more interesting ones but found myself drifting off into hypochondriac land again and quickly clicked off to the HA site (Hypochondriacs Anonymous). It's kind of ironic that it's called HA, as if someone is laughing at us. Are they? Am I being paranoid too?

Hypochondriacs Anonymous was formed by Herb Goldstein and Myron Klapowitz. Unfortunately the site is rarely updated as Herb and Myron are frequently out sick.

In South Florida there are expert hypochondriacs—lots of older people who live in retirement communities who can go on and on about many specific illnesses. They even refer to it as "Organ Recital" time (which is not when someone plays a piano) when people sit around a circle at the community pool, pick an organ (heart, lung, liver) and go through the diseases they have had associated with that organ, their friends have had with that organ, and information they have about diseases with that organ. Let's say the first time I was my visiting my parents and met their neighbors at the pool, they almost had to call an ambulance to cart me away. I was so looking forward to bingo or shuffleboard instead.

Life's cruel way of treating a hypochondriac is that it's a moving war against diseases. When you're a young, Jewish school-age hypochondriac, one red pimple certainly must mean the onslaught of chicken pox. One itch to the head and it must be an infestation of lice. As you move into the college years, you hope that burning sensation was simply hot coffee getting out of your system. In middle age, you start to worry about a whole new set of diseases. And as you enter the golden years, you actually see people getting sick and dying from those diseases. So at least at some point a Jewish male can safely say "You see, I wasn't being a hypochondriac."

One of the worst parts about being a hypochondriac is figuring out which meds to take, especially if you got your prescriptions from multiple doctors who really don't understand the interactions of the different drugs. And so many of the labels say that they "may cause drowsiness and **not** to operate heavy machinery." I have never driven a bulldozer, don't plan to, and can't imagine so many people need to be told not to when they take their meds!

I've typed so much today that I wonder if I'm getting carpal tunnel syndrome. Just a thought.

Color War & Bug Juice:
A Jewish Sleepaway

*Dinner was relatively uneventful though no one won the
"guess what kind of meat we just ate" contest.*

After completing my second year of college, I was trying
to figure out how I was going to spend my summer vacation.
Some of my friends were planning to travel around Europe,
others were getting intern jobs for really good money, and
others were going to their hometowns to spend time with
friends and family. I had not really planned for anything, as I
had been really busy at school partying.

I was a bit shocked when I got an invitation to be a Camp
Counselor near the Delaware River where I had been a camper
10 years before. My parents had sent an application in as they
thought it would be good for me and didn't want me sitting
home doing nothing. I flashed back to all the Jewish kids in
the neighborhood when I was growing up being sent off with
their giant green duffle bags. Was it for our enjoyment or for
a break for our parents?

Sleep-away camp was fun as a 9 year old, so I figured getting paid to go to camp was even better. I agreed to do it. It didn't take long to learn what a camp counselor's life is really like.

I assumed they paid minimum wage at least (plus tips) so I figured I would make at least $3,000 for the summer. As it turned out I was paid only $275 for the eight-week, 16-hours-a-day, seven-days-a-week job — which works out to 30 cents an hour. They told me that it was fair since they were paying for my room and board. As you'll soon hear, it was not like I was living at the Ritz-Carleton dining on lobster, so I begged to differ but to no avail. I had made more as a kid with my neighborhood lemonade stand.

Camp started on July 1st but new counselors had to come in for a couple of days of training prior to that. I arrived with my duffle bag, shoulder length hair, beard and red bandana across my forehead, and no clue what I was about to get myself into. Abe, the Head Counselor who gave us the basic rules of the camp and the proper ways to manage 10 year olds, trained us. I'm not sure Abe ever became well-known for child rearing but he had seniority. He also pointed me in the direction of the camp barber who transformed me from a hippie wannabe to an Abe look-alike. I trembled when I saw myself in the mirror with a crew cut. I had basically been drafted.

I was assigned as the counselor in the Squirrel bunk. One by one my campers arrived with their parents. I thought I was in the middle of the *Bad News Bears* as the variety of kids and parents floored me.

The Aaronburgs came first with young Ira, who had super-thick glasses and was tiny for his age. I could only think of how often he got beat up in his hometown.

Larry Lumpkin huffed and puffed his way up the three steps of the cabin with two half-eaten candy bars in one chocolate-covered hand and a big bag of candy as if he had just returned from a Halloween jaunt in the other. Mr. and Mrs. Lumpkin were huffing and puffing a few feet behind, also with mouths full of food. Mrs. Lumpkin, at least 100 pounds overweight, informed me that many people called Larry, "Lumpy," which she wanted me to prevent. "Sure, I said."

Shlomo Ginsberg was next and he was quite the sight. His parents were Orthodox Jews and they looked quite toasty in their black robes in the 100-degree heat. Shlomo had a yarmulke with a beret keeping it securely on his head. He also had a nebulizer in his left hand and a bag full of asthma and allergy medicine in his other. His parents said he was highly allergic to grass and dust so as I looked around the musty/dusty cabin and all the grass outside I couldn't help but wonder if they were trying to come up with some plan to sue the Camp. I could already tell that our bunk softball team was not going to win too many games.

The parents went on and on about the special needs of their kids and how I shouldn't forget what I was being told. Five more families arrived in the next few hours, including Dick (bed wetter), Bobby (hated to bathe), Johnny (anger management issues), Ricky (on Ritalin for hyperactivity) and twins (Terry and Tori) who appeared normal—at least relative to the others.

We all chose our bunks, put away our belongings, and got

to know each other a bit. Gradually the parents headed home and nine scared 10-year-olds were left with a shaved-head, beer-keg opening, margarita-making expert making 30 cents an hour who had absolutely no idea what to do next or for the next 55 days and 23 hours or so.

Just as I was beginning to panic, Abe got on the loud speaker and invited all campers to the main mess hall where we would be having dinner. We lined up along the path in bunk order (the Lions, Grizzlies, Tigers, etc.) along with us Squirrels. I tried to get Abe to switch our bunk name to something less meek but to no avail.

Dinner was relatively uneventful though no one won the "guess what kind of meat we just ate" contest. While the food was pretty inedible, it was good to see the two chocolate bars had not slowed down Lumpy (I mean Larry) from eating from most everyone else's unfinished plates. After dinner there was a big campfire, which was kind of neat though the smoke overtook poor Shlomo despite significant sucking in of his inhaler.

The sky was absolutely stunning—full of stars as we headed back to the Squirrels bunk for our first night of sleep. I couldn't wait to pass out. Lumpy (I mean Larry) passed out chocolate for the whole bunk, which had them all very wired past midnight—especially Ricky who was not supposed to get anywhere near food that fueled his hyperactivity. Scary stories were told and half the kids were so scared they wanted me to comfort them. Abe had not taught us how to do that and that basic character gene is not part of my natural DNA make-up. It was a long night made even worse when I forgot to remind

Dick the bed wetter to go the bathroom right before he went to bed. Naturally, his bed was located directly next to mine.

At 6:00 a.m. (precisely two hours after I had fallen asleep after changing Dick's smelly sheets), the speakers cranked out revelry, which was worse than any hangover wakeup. The Squirrels and I made it to breakfast without incident but were bummed when the mystery meat from last night was now part of an egg scramble. It was time to begin our first hike of the summer. I didn't know we were doing hikes at all. I had been looking forward to lounging on the dock or schmoozing with the hot arts & crafts teacher.

About two hours into the hike Lumpy (I mean Larry) and I almost collapsed from exhaustion and poor Shlomo was wheezing and sneezing like a 90-year-old man. At least his yarmulke was still on his head.

Little Ira was cruising along pretty well but he told me had to "make a number two." There were no facilities within miles so I led him into a bushy area where no one could see us. I figured I might as well do the same thing. We squatted down, did our thing and then realized we had no toilet paper. I told him confidently as if I had done this before, to grab those leaves over there and use them. (Growing up in New York City, I was a concrete guy not a plant guy, so I had no idea what I was suggesting to Ira). We both came out of the woods pulling our pants up. One of the other counselors, Howie, thought it was very weird to see a counselor and his camper pulling their pants up together coming out of the woods, and reported us to the head of the camp. That subsequent meeting was not pleasant.

We completed the hike and were thrilled to finally enjoy the beautiful lake. We swam for about an hour, got dried off, and headed off to lunch for some palette-cementing peanut butter sandwiches. I am still not sure why jelly was not an option as an adder to the sandwich. The interestingly named, disgusting "bug juice" drink they served round-the-clock made the choice of either drinking it to help loosen up the glue-like peanut butter, or die from choking, a tough decision.

As we got back to the bunk for our afternoon rest and postcard writing, Ira complained that his butt was beginning to itch really badly. I told him to lie on his stomach and relax as any non-trained 19-year-old might suggest. Fifteen minutes later he was scratching his butt like a swarm of mosquitoes were attacking him. I told him to pull down his pants and saw a rash like no other I had ever seen. I was putting some cortisone cream on him when Howie the camp-snitch walked in shaking his head. At the same time, I started getting the first inkling of my own butt itch. I was hoping I was just being a hypochondriac. Howie got closer to little Ira and told me it was definitely poison ivy. I quickly realized that those plant leaves I had used, and advised Ira to use, was far from the best choice. Within two more hours, both Ira and I had major swelling on our butts and right hand, and walked like we had been riding a horse for a month straight. We barely made it to the infirmary where they gave us some heavy-duty cream and Ira a shot, as his was really bad. The pain for me in trying to sit on a toilet and go to the bathroom over the next 2 days was indescribable. Ira stayed in bed for three days wishing he were home being beat up by the town bullies.

My first 24 hours was not going well as a leader. I got the first inkling that large dollar tips that the other counselors typically got at the end of summer was not something I should plan for. I kept on thinking how I was making 30 cents an hour and many of my friends were in Spain.

As my butt and hand got back to normal and summer rolled on, it actually became a bit enjoyable. As I became more and more hungry, the food didn't taste as bad as those first few days. I had the added benefit of having been subjected to college cafeteria food for the last two years. Even the bug juice somehow managed to make it down my throat after the head of the camp showed me how to drink it holding my fingers over my nostrils.

We canoed down the Delaware River as a group, which was a blast until most of the Squirrel canoes tipped over going through the rapids. I call them rapids but it was more like a slight one-second ripple. We needed to enhance the story to protect our dwindling Squirrel reputation.

We didn't do well athletically against the other bunks though my 10-year-olds did give the six-year-old Cub bunk a run for their money in flag football. We only lost by two touchdowns. Fortunately, our bunk was divided in half during Color War, so neither team got overly penalized.

Our panty raid (a camp tradition half-way through the summer) of the girls' bunks ended poorly as my boys (and truth be told me) got so excited when they were within arm's reach of the hanging panties on the outside clothesline, they (and I) began whooping and hollering like they (we) had found gold.

They had never seen real panties and frankly even as they got older, I always wondered if some of them ever did. One by one, screaming girls started coming out of their bunks and running our way. We were no match. Shlomo's yarmulke fell off as we began running away, Ira couldn't see well in the dark, and poor Lumpy ran like he had pocketfuls of jelly beans in his pants—which he did. Dick was so nervous he didn't wait until he got back to his bed to pee. The rest of our bunk tried to help the slower ones, and that's when the camp director caught us all.

The meeting that night did not go well and I was close to being fired. As I was getting yelled at, I thought of losing $275 and realized that at least I was not losing a lot of money. I thought of getting home to great food, which sounded wonderful. I thought of sleeping in my own bed at home, which sounded fantastic. I thought of hanging out with friends and family instead of nine Squirrels.

As the Camp Director was about to give me the ax, all the boys stood up as if on queue and begged the Camp Director to give me another chance. I was shocked. They actually told the Camp Director that I had taught them a lot (all I could think of was that they learned the dangers of poison ivy from me and how to make an armpit fart). For some reason, the Camp Director did give me that extra chance (in thinking back perhaps he couldn't find anyone to work for those slave wages). The final four weeks went well and I actually managed to get a few tips at the end, including one that perhaps I consider bartending the following summer.

2. No Pain, No Gain and No Stories

A S A NEAR-PROFESSIONAL COUCH potato, I have rarely had any misadventures watching sports on television and am quite good at it from years and years of experience. In fact I have been called a "great indoorsman" by those who know me well.

But even I have ventured into the world beyond my couch for various activities. As you will see, perhaps it was better to stay put and watch ESPN Ocho instead.

It's 120 Degrees—
Time for Yoga!

She grabbed me roughly by my wet shorts, snapped the waistband sharply on my hips, and told me that it would be best if I just sat in the hot room and skipped the exercises so that most of the toxins could still be released.

About 25 years ago I went on a cruise. Between the all-you-can-eat food and all-you-can-drink alcohol, my friends and I took a 30-minute yoga class. It was basically breathing and lying down. I was really good at the lying down part.

The other day my wife recommended I take yoga classes to improve my flexibility as she saw me doing less and less around the house, which was almost impossible given how little I typically had done in the past anyway. Off I went to the closest yoga studio figuring I could still lay down with the best of them.

There was a Sunday morning Hot Yoga class that began at 9:30 and was scheduled to end at 11:00. It seemed like a long time to lie down, breathe, say some ohmms and sniff incense, but I figured maybe there was a lecture thrown in as well.

I was told to get there early as a first-timer, so I got there about 20 minutes before the class was to officially begin. I was joined by three other first-timers. They looked a lot fitter than I was, which didn't really bother me as I bragged to them "I did yoga on a cruise 25 years ago." It didn't seem to make a difference to them.

The instructor looked so limber, even just walking, that she didn't look anything like the Spandex-busting, buffet-consuming yoga teacher from the cruise. She led us into a large room that looked like a typical workout room with giant mirrors all over the walls. The one thing that was noticeably different (even for someone like me who is not overly perceptive) was the 12 space heaters spread equally at the bottom of the walls cranked on high. We were told that the room was set at 105 degrees but it would get about 10-15 degrees hotter once the 40 people showed up for the class. Part of the theory of Hot Yoga is that the intense heat loosens the muscles and ligaments so you get the maximum stretch.

The three newbies and I sat down on our special mats (with shoes/socks off) to wait for the class to begin. By the time the class had assembled 15 minutes later, my shirt was completely drenched, I had finished my bottle of water, and I felt like I was close to passing out. I wasn't quite ready to begin a 90-minute anything. I can last about 10 minutes in a regular sauna; this was hotter and required movement unlike sitting in a sauna. As the people piled in, it did get hotter, which was almost impossible. The experienced people looked at us newbies with comforting faces and empathy for the torture we were about to endure. One guy whispered to me "If you don't puke in the first 30 minutes, consider yourself a successful beginner." With those encouraging words, the class was about to begin. I do think I heard "one more log for the fire" from the instructor. Most of the men were in these Speedo bathing suits, which was a bit much (actually a bit little) in my opinion.

My fellow newbies and I were put in the back row so we could watch the experts in front of us to learn the postures, not have the class laugh at us, and be as close to the heaters as possible. Not sure which was the main reason, but I have my suspicions.

I was directly behind this beautiful girl who in warm-ups put her left leg behind her right ear effortlessly while standing. She saw me sweating profusely, struggling to touch my shins as part of my warm-up. She said she had turned around as she thought she heard a whimper. I quickly pointed to the guy next to me and chuckled.

There was no incense, no lying down and no soft mystical music. It was 45 minutes of intense stretches, balancing standing up, followed by 45 minutes of exercises on one's back and stomach. I quickly earned the nickname of "Baby Flamingo" as I fell down about five times. My shirt was so wet it was actually making things seem heavier and harder. I took off my shirt, and that caused a few of my neighbors to move their mats a few feet away. It looked like the hot girl in front of me giggled but I was in such a mental fog I'm not quite sure. Thirty minutes into the class I started trying to decide whether it was better to puke in class or simply pass out. I decided to head for the exit to get some cold air. My legs weren't working so I began to crawl past heater after heater, which gave me quite the unexpected sunburn and knee burns. I was so happy that the teacher hadn't locked the doors and I was able to escape. After about five minutes of pure joy (breathing), the instructor found me inside the cooler of cold drinks sniffing furiously.

She grabbed me roughly by my wet shorts, snapped the waistband sharply on my hips, and told me that it would be best if I just sat in the hot room and skipped the exercises so that most of the toxins could still be released. I told her, in a child-like pleading voice, that I thought most of the toxins were already gone and that I promised I would never put another toxin into my body again.

She told me that the other newbies were still hanging in there, so she wanted me to try to continue. Against my better judgment I crawled back in and continued with the class. I was astonished to see so many people who could do amazing contortions with their bodies. Where were these girls when I was in college? Even some of the older guys were pretty limber. One guy took me under his wing and said he was even worse than I was when he started 10 months ago. I said "Really?" He said, "Well, almost as bad." I had filled up my water bottle and was drinking it as much as I could but it was so hot in the room it felt like the water was evaporating before it even hit my mouth.

I looked up at the clock and there were only 18 minutes left in the class. I had calculated I had about 20 minutes of life left in my body so I prayed the class wouldn't go long. Whimpering like a wounded puppy (I tried to be quiet about it but a few people were staring at me and not because they wanted to learn how to do a certain posture). I pushed myself until only three minutes were left. I had sweated so much that there simply was no more sweat that could come out. Somehow I made it to the end of the class, but I was stuck. On one hand, my body was so tired I could not get off the mat; I was one with the mat and as flat as it. On the other hand, through my dazed state I saw others gathering their belongings and heading for the cold air of the office. I stayed on that mat for about five minutes trying to drink out of my bottle lying completely flat, which was a sad sight. I was just hoping I wasn't going to drown. I finally managed to gather my soaking wet towels, my mat, my water bottle, my sneakers, my socks and my drenched shirt and hobbled over to the escape hatch. I looked like a homeless person with their meager possessions. The beautiful girl who barely looked like she broke a sweat said, "Nice job, Cruise Boy." I told her through parched lips that if I hadn't gotten to class 20 minutes early I could have kept up with her. I think she's still laughing.

I paid the office attendant and she asked me when I would be back. She recommended I come back tomorrow to "maximize my oxidation and my spine stretch." I told her I was busy tomorrow as I was going to be at the hospital getting an IV.

Thinking the worst was over as I headed to my car, I forgot how a black car (brilliant color choice by me) tends to heat up quite a bit in the summertime in Florida. After fumbling for my car keys, as my fingers seemed like they had atrophied, I managed to get the door open and throw in my wet stuff. Somehow I bent down and got into my car which not only was hotter than the class I just escaped but the leather seat against my wet bare back gave new meaning to the phrase "searing heat." I turned the air-conditioning on as fast as I could full blast, and after a few minutes the car was at a reasonable temperature. My legs were still wobbly so driving home was quite the adventure. As I glided through a couple of stop signs as I couldn't quite get my leg working the brake, I prayed that I wouldn't get pulled over. I wasn't wearing a shirt, shoes or socks, just a soaking wet pair of shorts pulled up so high it almost looked like a thong. Plus the air-conditioning vent was turned directly on my wet shorts. A cop might have wondered what the heck was going on. And if he asked me to step out of the car that might have been the end.

I made it to my driveway and uncorked myself from my car, as my body seemed stuck in the sitting up position. Again fumbling with my keys I got through the front door, barely made it to the bedroom, and collapsed there for two hours. What woke me up was the squishing sound below me as I had somehow managed to sweat out a few more pints just lying there. I felt like a grape that had just turned into a raisin.

That night my sore lower back actually felt better, but I think it was because every other muscle in my body was unbelievably sore in comparison. They say the pain is worst the next day—I could hardly wait to wake up in the morning.

DO-OVER

Growing up one could use the word do-over for almost anything. Like striking out in a backyard baseball game or throwing two consecutive gutter balls in bowling or failing a spelling test (not that all of those examples have happened to me, at least not that I can remember well). I have not used the do-over phrase in 35 years but it seems appropriate now.

After a grueling week of going through four tubes of Ben Gay, two Epsom salt baths and three massages to help my incredibly sore muscles, I decided to see if I could beat Yoga as it had clearly dominated me last week. No one who knows me thought I would do Yoga the first time and clearly no one thought I would try it again. That group included me as well. I wanted a do-over.

I decided I needed a new plan to try and win:

1) Instead of going to the second class of the day when the heaters had already been cranking for three hours and the class was packed with 40 people, I decided to go to the "crack of dawn" class thinking the heaters would not yet be at full blast and there would be less body heat.

2) Instead of waiting to drink water during the class after I had sweated out pints and was dizzy from dehydration, I would drink a ton of water before class.

3) Instead of arriving 20 minutes early as a first-timer
    and pre-frying in the sauna-like room waiting for
    others to arrive, I would show up one minute before
    the class was to actually begin.

I arrived at 6:59 on a Saturday morning. Most humans
were still in bed, except for the five male Indians and me.
There were no pretty girls like last week. The Indians looked
like they had attended Yogi Masters in Training for the last
15 years, and they were in phenomenal shape. These people
looked like they might have worked at circuses as human
pretzels getting in and out of tiny boxes. I was tired from
walking up the steps to the second floor workout studio and
I looked like I had previous employment as a taste-tester
at a pastry shop. I was really bummed there were no other
completely inflexible people in the class.

I had a new teacher this time. Her name was Helga and
I believe her resume included a brief stint as a Marine drill
instructor. The five Indians who had been stretching in the
heated sauna 20 minutes before class nodded a quick hello
as I entered the room. Compared to last time, it was not as
hot, only a stifling 105 degrees instead of 120. We were about
to begin when I raised my hand and asked if I could go the
bathroom as the one gallon of water I drank around 6:30 was
not sitting well with me. Helga was not pleased and said that
if I had to go again I would need to wait until there was a
break between one of the 30 postures.

I returned with stares from Helga and the five "Boys from Bombay." During the early part of the 90 minutes, I was able to kick the broiling space heater so it faced the guy that looked like Gandhi the most, instead of it facing me. Helga caught on to that about 15 minutes later and pointed it directly at me. I was sweating like Ben Stiller in *Along Came Polly* when he was eating the really spicy Indian food.

We stretched into positions not humanly possible. Well, at least they did. Helga came over and manually tried to move different parts of my body, but my 48 years of rigidness proved much tougher than even Helga.

It started getting really hot so I cleverly unplugged the heater closest to me with my right leg. It's amazing how far one can really stretch if there is a clear purpose. Another 15 minutes went by before Helga caught me. I told her it was an accident but she was onto me for sure and definitely did not believe me.

I continued to guzzle water and Gatorade as puddles and puddles of sweat were forming on my rubber mat. I wondered in my semi-hallucinatory state whether I could drown in one inch of water. I really needed to go to the bathroom but the class was not at a stopping point, so I created my own posture with knees bent in, groin tight, and a grimace on my face. Helga came over (one disadvantage of being in a class with six people instead of 40 is that it's impossible to hide) and asked me what yoga teacher had ever taught me that pose. I told her I learned it at a rock concert when I was stuck in a port-a-john line and everyone had been drinking beer all day. She had no idea what I was talking about and since I was close to losing control, I hopped on out the door in my posture. I don't think they're going to make that a new pose, but trust me it was a difficult one. One of the Indians said something in Hindu that must have meant something along the lines of "The hopping Easter Bunny is about to spring a leak" as all the others laughed. I returned again in about five minutes to the dismay of the class. Helga loudly asked if I had a bladder problem and I said "Not until this morning."

The 90-minute class was half over and I hadn't puked or passed out (I think the trips to the bathroom were nice breaks for me) so I was feeling relatively cocky. There was only lying down postures remaining (as opposed to the one-legged balancing ones seemingly juggling sharp knives at the same time) one of which required laying on one's back pulling both knees up to the chest and then lifting the pelvis as high as you could. According to the teacher, this posture was supposed to "massage the lower ascending colon, release trapped gas and move the bubbles around."

I couldn't get my knees to touch my chest and they weren't quite perfectly positioned over my hips, so Helga decided to torture me again. She was down by my feet and grabbed my knees and pushed them as hard as she could, ramming them into my chest while yelling at me to breathe in deeply as she was doing this. I told her in a staggered voice " this—is— very—painful" but she said the pain would go away if I kept on breathing in and out in the exact technique I had been taught in the first five minutes of class. I believe I was out of the room at that time having my own blissful moment. Feeling not much relief, she said that I should take one really deep breath and then hold it. I did that and she pushed my knees apart and even more into my chest. Helga was so close to me I could literally see the evil in her eyes. I was not happy and couldn't believe I had paid for this pain. I was wishing I could stop my do-over.

She said the next thing I should do was "Expel your wind." I started letting the breath out of my mouth and she said it louder, "Expel *all* your wind." Without going into the details as to exactly what happened next with my trapped gas, suffice it to say Helga is no longer so helpful to others with that posture.

Head down, I gathered my belongings (I left my soaking mat as I wouldn't ever need it in the future and it was too heavy anyway at this point) and left while being stared at by five sweaty Indians in Speedos and a German woman wondering if she would teach yoga again.

After going to yoga twice and asking various friends to try some of the postures, I am convinced that the average person is quite inflexible and that the people who do yoga are extremely unusual people. With that in mind, I am thinking of starting the "Goldberg Stiff-As-A-Board Yoga School" for people who can't bend well, who don't like to get nauseous, and who can't follow directions when told to "grab your right foot instep, while it's pointed to the left, with your left hand turned upside down after putting it under the knee while standing on your left leg that is bent at a 45-degree angle."

In the end I'm not sure if I beat yoga or not, but I would say I got "two legs up" on Helga. And somewhere there are five Indians telling their buddies about their most unusual day at yoga class.

Organically Surprised

Next we stopped and got some eggs from "happy chickens fed with a high omega-3 diet." I didn't know how they knew the chickens were happy but I was too afraid to ask. Later when I saw the chickens in the pre-cooked rotisserie section, I didn't sense they were all too happy to be contributing.

Almost everyone I know has been on a diet at one time. If I had lost only one pound for each of the diets I've tried over the years, I'd be at a perfect weight. Or if I suddenly had a growth spurt of six inches at age 50, I would be at a fine weight as well. However, somewhere over the years, about 20-25 pounds have found themselves nestled on my frame—much of it forming a lovely (at least to me) circular band around my waist.

Against that backdrop, I was home one Saturday lying on my couch, eating my wonderful lunch of packaged bologna on white bread with processed American cheese, a large bag of salted potato chips, and a value-sized 32-ounce soda. Life was good and I was saving money with my value-sized drink.

Plus I was only a few minutes away from rewarding myself with one of my favorite desserts, a yodel topped with whipped cream and chocolate sprinkles—a "Chocolate Splatter"as my son Michael named it.

I heard a knock on the door and was bummed when my "Come In!' scream from the couch was not heard over the television, and I actually had to get up and go to the door. A man claiming to be my neighbor from two houses down (I don't socialize much on my street and I don't do much yard work) was at the door. He was coming over to see if we had any soymilk that he could borrow.

Clearly we had no such thing in the house, but I did offer him a piece of my yodel concoction. He politely refused and started to walk away when I noticed his "stomach tire'" was missing from the one other time I had met him. He actually had a real body—well at least one different than mine. I told him to come in and tell me what he'd been doing to lose the weight, since I'd much prefer looking for magical ideas versus simply eating less and exercising more.

He told me that about three months ago he had changed his lifestyle (not "gone on a diet") and had basically given up anything with refined sugar (ice cream, cookies, crackers, white rice, white bread, most packaged foods, processed cheeses, soda, etc.) and completely focused on eating whole foods—vegetables, fruits, nuts, seeds, eggs, lean meats, etc.

I was shocked that people could survive on real food. I looked down at my lunch and shook my head in disbelief that Americans could live on whole foods. He told me to try it for a week and that I would feel great and lose weight. I ordered a sausage pizza for dinner with extra cheese, finished off my last couple of bottles of soda, and thought about what he said. After finishing my last quart of premium ice cream, I decided to give it a whirl.

It was about 7:00 p.m., and I gathered my whole family around. I wanted to show them that I was committed to doing this. I announced: "As of now, I'm changing my lifestyle."

My oldest son asked flippantly, "Does that mean you are going to do chores around the house now?" My youngest son asked nervously, "You're not moving in with a man are you?" My wife just stared at me, not having a clue as to what I was trying to say or do.

I explained to them what I was planning on doing, and they pretty much mocked me and went back to their Hershey Bars and Fruit Roll-ups.

Off I ventured to the nearby health foods supermarket to begin my new lifestyle. When I drove into the parking lot I was shocked at just how big the store was and how packed the parking lot was. Maybe real food was actually being eaten by a lot of people!

As I got to the front window display, I saw things like "Organic Wild Alaskan Salmon, $22/lb," "Quinoa, only $2," "Tofu Surprise, $6.99." These signs were so different from my regular supermarket specials of "Twinkies $1.99," and "Buy two 64-oz. bottles of soda and get a 3rd free" or "Frosted, Sugar Puffy Pops Cereal, now with a mini chocolate bar inside."

I walked in and was immediately struck by the sheer number of giant, color-exploding fruits and vegetables right at the front of the store. My normal supermarket has a 12-foot display of marshmallow packages as soon as you walk in.

The store was huge and I couldn't tell what was behind the giant pineapple section or the tables of beautiful mangos, so I tiptoed in the direction of the other departments as if not wanting anyone to see this sugar-enriched human who I felt all healthy eyes were about to descend on. I was actually nervous.

A way-too-happy, super-healthy looking worker (not like the grumpy old, fat guys and pimply-faced teens at my regular supermarket) came over to me and asked if I needed any help. I guess I looked dazed. He seemed very bright as well; he must be using that Ginkgo Biloba stuff advertised throughout the store.

I told him I needed a basic plan since I was changing my lifestyle. First he took me to the 50 giant plastic dispensers of beans, nuts, seeds, and dried fruit. You pull on a giant handle and out come things you've never heard of into a plastic bag. The only thing I had seen remotely similar to this was during my trip to Dylan's Candy Bar in Manhattan where you can fill up from giant dispensers with Good N' Plenty, Charleston Chews, Sugar Babies and Necco Wafers. I wasn't sure if my Mung Beans, Steel Cut Oat Groats and Golden Flax Seeds were going to taste as good as Dylan's candy. Isn't there fiber in Necco Wafers?

Next we stopped and got some eggs from "happy chickens fed with a high omega-3 diet." I didn't know how they knew the chickens were happy but I was too afraid to ask. Later when I saw the chickens in the pre-cooked rotisserie section, I didn't sense they were all too happy to be contributing.

After putting in my cart some great looking fresh vegetables, he told me that I should still think about getting a product called Veggie Wash that removes any type of pesticide, oil, etc. Since I wanted to break my 50-year-old habit of eating pesticides (maybe I would run like the wind or something), I figured what the heck and added it.

We then picked up some Wild Alaskan salmon, organic chickens (they didn't brag about what state they were from) and "hand-stroked" beef. Now that's a job I missed out on growing up.

In the cereal section, my helper guy suggested a box of Amarenth Flakes that he said tasted great with soy milk. I was so excited I could hardly wait until the next morning. I almost asked him for a bowl so I could try it right there.

As we were heading to the cash register, he said that if I really wanted to get the full effect of feeling my best I should get some all-natural toothpaste and some vitamins/supplements. Feeling plucky, I agreed. He chose a toothpaste that said "All-Natural Sea Algae CoQ10." I couldn't imagine too many worse sounding things to put in my mouth, but his teeth looked bright and shiny so I went with the flow. The last purchase was a multivitamin and an Omega-3 supplement.

I emptied my cart, the woman at the register rang me up, and then I emptied my wallet. It's amazing how much more expensive real food is versus processed food. You would think it would be the opposite.

When I got home I swallowed my first, super-enriched multivitamin and wondered if I would feel something wonderful in the next few minutes. I did not of course, but in my own warped brain I was on my way to feeling great and looking better.

I then opened the extra large jar of Omega-3 fish oil supplements and began to panic. I was supposed to swallow two of these capsules per day. They were so big they looked more like suppositories. And someone at the Omega-3 factory must have had a great sense of humor because they were shaped like swordfish. After sucking on the first one for 15 minutes trying to get the capsule down, I was bummed when the fish oil started leaking out into my mouth. I'm not sure exactly how they get fish oil out of a fish in the first place, or how they then get it into the capsule, but the one thing I am now quite clear about is that you absolutely do not want this liquid substance opening anywhere but your stomach—fully encapsulated.

I ran to the sink to suck down some water when I realized that I was supposed to be drinking the special ultra-purified water I just bought from the health foods store. Four dollars of water later, I had finally gotten rid of most of the horrible taste. That was my last fish oil supplement. I decided that eating grilled salmon and scrambled eggs (special Omega-3 enriched ones from happy chickens) was far more palatable.

I've been on this diet, I mean lifestyle change, for about two months now. I've lost 15 pounds and I'm feeling good. Not sure if the multivitamin benefits have kicked in yet but damn it, I've ingested over $120 of vitamins so far. Somewhere inside of me that must be paying off.

I am no longer nervous when I enter the health food store and actually know some of the workers there now. I even help the new shoppers who have that "deer in the headlights" look to learn about the world of real foods. Hand-stroked deer, that is.

Do I miss my yodel with whipped cream and sprinkles? Do I miss my bologna sandwiches? Do I miss my potato chips and Rocky Road ice cream? You bet I do. But there's something about an organic mango smoothie, made with ice cubes from ultra-purified water, that tastes pretty darn good. I do wonder sometimes if they can make organic Sugar Daddy's or organic Pez.

Doing the Slopes

After getting outfitted by a very patient teenager, I stumbled my way out of the shop swinging my poles and skis wildly and narrowly missing guillotining a few people.

I'm not into heights and not into cold weather (especially after living in South Florida for the last 25 years) so clearly going to the top of a mountain, over a 500-foot ravine on a chair lift in the middle of the winter is not at the top of my list to try.

However, when best friends like Tom and Doug call and tell you it'll be a lot of fun at night even if you don't ski, I decided to take the plunge. The destination was Aspen, Colorado, a truly picturesque place.

Here's what really happens to out-of-shape, middle-aged first timers.

Prior to our mid-January trip, I realized that my typical attire of tee shirts, shorts and/or bathing suit was not going to be sufficient. While I hate shopping in general, I dragged myself to the local store and stocked up, as I had virtually nothing.

Warm coat, long underwear, turtlenecks, warm socks, gloves, mittens, hats, earmuffs, sweaters, etc. were all purchased with the hope that I would use them again beyond this one trip, as the cost of the stuff was more than the plane ticket.

We arrived in Aspen on a Friday afternoon on the coldest day in the last 15 years. I remember leaving the airport and realizing there was almost a 100-degree temperature change between what I left in Florida and what I arrived to in Colorado. My friends comforted me by telling me that, if I did decide to ski, the top of the mountain would be even colder and windier.

We checked into our condo and then went directly to one of the local bars as people were ending their skiing for the day and taking part in après ski—after-skiing partying. I was inside the bar and wearing what seemed like everything I had brought with me on the trip, including 2 shirts, 2 sweaters and a jacket as I was freezing. I looked like I was 20 pounds heavier than I was and pretty stupid looking in hindsight, as no else seemed to be that bothered by the cold. I proceeded to have some drinks and pretty soon I was down to one shirt and one sweater, looking relatively normal and feeling quite relaxed.

We seamlessly moved from happy hour to nighttime partying—I was really enjoying the ski trip.

At about 1:00 a.m., it was time to head back to the condo. After 15 minutes of putting my layers of clothes back on, we skidded our way back to the condo. My friends told me it was time for a trip to the Jacuzzi so we got into our bathing suits and jumped into the outdoor condo Jacuzzi. It was about 100 degrees in the Jacuzzi but minus 20 degrees out of it. There's nothing quite like being wet in minus 20 degree weather. I must admit it did remove any feeling of drunkenness.

We got back to the condo, turned on the fireplace and talked a bit more until we fell asleep around 3:00 a.m. At 6:00, I heard our neighbors making all kinds of noise. They wanted to be one of the first skiers on the slopes. My two buddies were ready and raring to go. I was thoroughly enjoying my electric blanket and was not ready to go, though trying to get in the spirit of it. I jumped in the shower, turned the water on and got blasted with freezing water. I was now wide awake.

My friends were expert skiers. Double-black diamond runs were no problem for them. I told them I would catch up with them later. I had found out that of the four main ski areas in Aspen, Tiehack was supposed to be the easiest so I headed over there and decided to give skiing a chance. The real name of Tiehack is Buttermilk, but I just couldn't admit that was the name of the mountain I was skiing—it sounded like a place for pansies. I was really bummed when my one-week lift ticket attached to my jacket boldly had the word "Buttermilk" on it in giant lettering—it just as well could have said "loser."

I got to the mountain and went to the rental shop to get my skis, boots and poles. After getting outfitted by a very patient teenager, I stumbled my way out of the shop swinging my poles and skis wildly and narrowly missing guillotining a few people.

My next choice was which chairlift to take. As I fell face first with my skis spread apart as far as they could possibly be (quite the pull on the groin/hamstrings, I must admit) I managed to get up and repeat that fall about one minute later. Oh, how I wished I hadn't failed yoga. Some little kid felt bad for me as he thought I was physically disabled and helped get me up. He told me that I looked like a "pre-beginner." I had never heard that low of a category in reference to anything. He recommended I start with the rope tow.

I looked over at the rope tow area and saw about 50 five-year olds and was almost too proud to join them, but I figured I would do it once and then be on my way to the chairlifts and then the gondolas.

Somehow I got over to the rope tow area and got in line behind all the kids in their cute outfits. My outfit was not quite put together in any color coordination, I smelled of alcohol, and had a five-day beard growth, so I wasn't particularly welcomed by the ski instructors or the parents in color-coordinated outfits coaxing their kids. I looked eerily similar to the man in the poster under the heading "Stay Away from Strangers" that was in the kiddie section of the main lodge.

I positioned myself for the rope, grabbed on, and held on super tight for the one-minute trip up the hill. I somehow managed to make it down the hill and only took out a few kids on my wipeouts. They cried and complained to the ski instructors that "big people should not be on the kiddie hill." I spent the rest of the day perfecting getting up via the rope tow and down the hill. I was pretty proud of myself.

I made it back to the condo and my friends were telling

tales about skiing down unbelievably steep slopes and through tree-lined paths at incredible speeds. They also told me about all the cool people they met in the gondolas. I told them that I was at the top of Tiehack mountain skiing some blues and even a couple of blacks. They were impressed.

We went out to dinner that night at a local family-friendly restaurant and on the way my buddies noticed that my gloves were ripped to shreds like I had been holding onto a rope all day. I told them I was skiing down a black diamond slope and fell into some tree branches where my gloves got ripped. They claimed they had never seen branches do that to gloves. They were also surprised to see rope-like burns on my hands, but they soon forgot about it.

Dinner was going well until I heard "There's that big kid, Mr. Arnie" from across the room. I was hoping that there was another person who skied the kiddie hill all day who told the people to call him "Mr. Arnie," but alas it was I alone. Five-year-old Cindy and seven-year-old Bobby came running over to say hi and asked if their snowplowing tips had helped me. My buddies were not sure what was going on. I told the kids that they must be mistaking me with someone else but they pointed to my Buttermilk ski ticket, my rope-burned hands and my purple pants with a bright green turtleneck (the kids had told me all day I looked like a very non-athletic Barney the dinosaur), and said they were quite sure I was the guy that skied with them on the bunny hill all day (actually, until I got tired two hours into it and needed to stop for the rest of the day).

BOLITHO.

I was busted and mocked for the rest of the night and the rest of the trip by my buddies. I went to the local spa the next day instead of skiing and really enjoyed the massage, the facial, the wraps, etc. and concluded that while I may be a pre-beginner skier, I was quite the expert at relaxation and après ski. The rest of the week went great, as I became well known at the spas and bars in town. I had given my lift ticket away.

At the airport I was well-rested and getting ready to board for the long trip back from Colorado to Florida when I heard, "Mr. Arnie, Mr. Arnie." It was another group of young kids I had met that first day of skiing (I was surprised I made such an impression). They were going to be on the same plane and were sitting right behind my group of friends and me. They were only too happy to share stories about Mr. Arnie's first day on the bunny hill with my double-black diamond friends. My friends laughed all the way back to Florida.

I tried to return all my ski apparel to the store claiming they must have been broken, but to no avail. My friends are going back this year to Aspen. I'm thinking of going to Disney World with Cindy and Bobby and their parents.

Fore!

Everyone was having a blast and the beer-cart girl was getting rich.

There's nothing quite like getting out and playing 18 holes of golf with good friends with a beautiful, bikini-clad girl driving a golf cart around selling ice-cold beers.

I decided to organize a neighborhood outing for 20 guys. We had all talked about doing it for months, but nothing was happening, as we were all kind of waiting around for someone else to do something. It was not a big surprise that 20 guys couldn't get their act together.

I called a number of golf courses and as I knew, playing golf in Florida in the winter months is very expensive. That's the time of year we warmly welcome the tourists from up north, from their below zero degree temperatures, and while they are still defrosting we rip them off with high prices at restaurants, hotels and golf courses. It's our way of saying thank you for not having a state tax in Florida.

As I reported back to the troops, no one wanted to pay $100 for a round of golf as most of these guys were pure hackers and had played more courses with little windmills and clown's noses than real golf courses.

It turns out that once all the planes are filled with sunburned visitors exiting our Sunshine State, the prices begin to decline starting in May. As the hottest days of the year approach, the prices come down to their lowest point. So we chose June 21st, the first day of summer to play our little tournament. We also decided that we would start playing at noon since we could save an extra $2 per person. What a deal! It turned out that by choosing to play at noon we were subjected to a starting temperature of 95 degrees with absolutely no wind and 90% humidity. What a decision!

All was going well. We had split into five teams mixed with good players and some miniature golf experts. I was with Bob, a good golfer, Dr. Mike, a great doctor who was the only doctor I ever met who somehow never managed to get out and play golf, and Big Roman (6' 4", 250 pounds), a Czech neighbor who had never played before but enjoyed bumping his cart into other teams' carts, which came in handy as the competition heated up.

I have played golf, or more precisely tried to play golf, since I was eight years old, so you would think that after 40 plus years I would have figured out how to play well. I have all the excuses down pat (golf clubs bad, hung over, too windy, grass too wet, group in front too slow, rough too deep, sand traps not well kept, greens too tilted, ball with crack in it, etc.). I always manage to shoot about 95-100, assuming I only mildly cheat.

After the first six holes, I was actually hitting the ball quite well and putting much better than normal. Everyone was having a blast and the beer-cart girl was getting rich. By the time we finished the first nine holes and stopped to get something to eat, I was feeling a little woozy but assumed it was just a blast from the heat or from all the driving I was doing trying to chase the beer girl and her refreshments. By now it was 98 degrees and the humidity was higher as well. On the 14th green (the furthest green from the clubhouse of course) I was lining up a putt and literally collapsed from the heat. My group was scared, though having an ER doctor as your cart-mate turned out to be a good selection on my part (even though he was well on his way to a score of about 150 with almost as many balls lost).

They hauled my semi-conscious body into the cart and Mike drove as fast as the cart could go. They got me to the clubhouse about 10 minutes later and by this point I'm told I was completely unconscious. They laid me down in the clubhouse and immediately covered me in ice and wet towels. I was not responding so they called an ambulance that arrived five minutes later. They tried all kinds of things to revive me but I was out cold and they were very concerned.

I was later told that Dr. Mike leaned over to me and announced that he was going to perform CPR on me. I'm not sure if it was just perfect timing or some latent homophobic fear, but my eyes opened for the first time in about 20 minutes with Mike's mouth aiming for mine. Everyone was happy to see my eyes open, especially Mike.

I was rushed to the hospital, given intravenous fluids, and started to feel better in a couple of hours. They diagnosed me as having a ketosis reaction from being on a very low-carb diet and not getting enough carbs and the right kind of fluids into my body in the intense heat. I decided to go off the diet that day.

I also finally broke 85 that day (albeit I only played 14 holes). I guess I did learn that a low-carb diet can help lower one's golf score. I also told Dr. Mike that if that scary thing every happened again to me, that he should get the bikini-clad, beer-selling girl to attempt the CPR.

3. Raw Fish, Raw Deal

I MOVED TO TOKYO FOR three years on a job assignment with Motorola, which opened a whole new land of embarrassing opportunities.

It was quite the risky adventure as I didn't speak a word of Japanese, hated the thought of sushi, wasn't into crowds, was deathly afraid of earthquakes, had never traveled out of the U.S. and didn't know a single person who lived there. But I thought I could at least be the dominating center in basketball that I had always dreamed of: "Shaq" Goldberg.

I remember getting off the plane for the first time after the 20-hour, multi-stop flight from Ft. Lauderdale, Florida to Tokyo and thinking, "How do you say holy sh*t in Japanese?"

Arriving in Japan Clueless

How much worse could my luck be if I couldn't get any action from a porn star? I could see her naked on my TV but not in person in front of my TV.

The JAL (Japan Airlines) plane was filled with passengers prepared for this long trip as we taxied on the runway. A Japanese stewardess gave her speech over the intercom in both Japanese and English. I never did understand why the safety instructions on the plane in Japanese were 10 minutes long with a lot of animated explanations, while the English translation was simply "In case of a crash, put your head down and pray." I felt like I was missing out on some key details. As it turned out, no one filled me in on a lot of key details before I was basically dropped off in a foreign country. However, I was ready to be on the lookout for new things.

After getting through Customs, I was greeted by one of the Nippon Motorola (the Japanese subsidiary of my U.S. company) secretaries at the airport. She spoke very little English, so it was a quiet two-hour bus ride to Tokyo. All I remembered from my Japanese audiotape lessons was how to say "This bus is yellow," which didn't quite fill up the two hours. Plus the bus was gray.

The company arranged for me to stay in a hotel in Shinjuku (across the street from the relatively unknown, very bizarre sex district of Tokyo). Given what I was seeing on a nightly basis (mostly from straining my neck from the window of my hotel), I did not rush in my hunt to find an apartment. My stereotypical view was of Japanese people bowing a lot and taking lots of pictures while traveling in groups. The sex district had groups, but they weren't bowing or taking pictures.

At the young age of 27, I was in put in charge of the Japanese marketing department in Tokyo, and since I was younger than most of my employees (seniority is a big deal in Japan) I was instantly disliked. I may not have been liked if I was 86 years old either, but who knows. The fact that it was tough via hand signals (since most of them spoke no English) to indicate "I need a business analysis of the cell phone competition by Thursday" made it that much more frustrating for both sides. It was like playing charades for 12 hours a day, five days a week, and rarely having the joy of touching your nose saying, "Yes, you got it."

Over time, I did manage to learn some Japanese. At least my Japanese teachers told me I was learning and encouraged me to keep paying their exorbitant fees. None of the people at work understood any of my words. Thus, I'm not quite sure if I really learned it or not. Perhaps it was my New York-accented-Japanese that didn't quite come out correctly or the fact that most of my Japanese sentences began with "Yo."

While it was certainly a wonderful experience, it was often a very stressful experience. It was never a huge desire for me to meet lots of new people, as I had a small group of tight-knit friends in the U.S. So trying to meet single women in Japan when I first arrived without speaking Japanese was really a tough challenge. It probably would have been difficult even if I was fluent given my below average hit-rate in the U.S. It was unfortunate, since my company had rented this big apartment for me and it would have been a good place to have parties.

It was impossible to meet anyone at work where most of my time was spent. Of the 100 people at our Japanese subsidiary, there were 90 Japanese men, five American men and five married Japanese women who served green tea all day to the 95 men. Slavery was alive and well in Japan.

Going out to bars was tricky as the language barrier was a huge issue in the hundreds of small, local bars. The fancy "club" bars, where English was prevalent, were only open to the "special" "A-list" people such as rich Japanese businessmen, models, actors, and rock stars.

After about three months of not really meeting anyone, even though I was living with 10 million other people, I dragged myself one night to the one "foreigner" place, the Tokyo Hard Rock Café. There were about 20 stools around the bar and one empty one, so I sat down and ordered my Jack Daniels & water. Not that I was eavesdropping or anything, but I overheard a cute Japanese-looking girl next to me complaining in English (New York English to boot) to someone sitting next to her.

She was not having a great time in Japan, as she had recently moved here from New York to live with her aunt to get a better sense for her ancestry but felt like she had little freedom to go out and didn't like living in a small apartment. I ordered another drink for myself and then I believe one more for enhanced courage.

I think I tapped her on the shoulder 20 minutes later and slurred something like "I didn't hear everything you were saying but would you like to move into my apartment for a couple of weeks and take care of my dog while I go to Florida for business, and if it works out you can live with me for free for three years?" I couldn't tell when she turned around, eyes and mouth agape, whether this was the boldest, strangest thing she had heard or just a good idea. In hindsight, I think it was a little bit of both.

She said OK, after thinking about it for 20 seconds (she was doing her own share of drinking), and we figured since we might be living together for three years we might as well know each other's names. She was Amy (in fact she still is Amy) and yes, for three years she was my roommate in Tokyo and we became best of friends. She was well connected in town, super cool, and introduced me to a ton of people and places. If it weren't for that chance encounter at the Hard Rock Café and that one open barstool, who knows what my time in Japan would have been like, or hers.

I always laugh at how Amy introduced me to one of her acquaintances who was an "up and coming" Japanese porn star. She recently released a few XXX movies. She liked my New York accent and liked to learn English from me, but nothing else. How much worse could my luck be if I couldn't get any action from a porn star? I could see her naked on my TV but not in person in front of my TV.

I must admit Amy did almost get me evicted from my apartment and almost killed, but except for those two things, she was a great roommate and friend. The near-eviction happened the first week she had moved in and the near-death experience happened near the end of the third year (more on that story in a later chapter...)

When I left for Florida on the business trip right after meeting her, I told Amy to enjoy the apartment and to just make sure she walked the dog a few times a day. My company housed their few American employees in Japan in very nice apartments so that they wouldn't complain about the exorbitantly high prices of everything, the stifling crowds, never seeing their American friends or families in the U.S., the inability to communicate, etc. I lived on the top floor in a large place with only one neighbor on my floor, the President of Louis Vuitton. He was a very quiet, distinguished family man who liked the fact that I knew no one and had no visitors.

I called Amy from Florida on a Saturday morning (Saturday night Japan time) which was only three days removed from the Hard Rock Café encounter. I expected to hear the television on or maybe my dog barking, but instead I heard noises like there was a band playing and hundreds of people in the house. I hung up thinking I must have dialed the wrong number. I called back and there was that same band. I could barely make out Amy's voice but she had decided to throw a "Welcome Amy" party for herself and about 50 of the A-list people in Tokyo. I was amazed that she was doing it and amazed she could pull it off with only a few days notice. She stammered a bit and said the dog was really doing well. I hung up in disbelief.

I made it back to Tokyo about 10 days later and all the furniture had been rearranged, there were new plants in the house, and new pictures on the wall. I thought I was in the wrong apartment. My dog was very happy to see me. Now if only dogs could talk.

Amy apologized for the blowout party without me but I let it go thinking, "Wow, maybe these people will actually show up when I'm around." I hadn't been home more than 15 minutes, extremely tired from jet lag when I heard a loud banging on the door. It was my neighbor and the apartment building superintendent. The super started yelling at me in Japanese, which was fine since I had no idea what he was saying. I didn't learn any of those words in my Japanese language classes. Mr. Louis Vuitton gave it to me loudly in English and wondered what was going on in my apartment when I was gone. He complained that all these lingerie-model types were prancing in and out of the apartment over the two weeks I was gone and demanded that this activity stop. "Stop?" I said, "Over my dead body," which may have not been the right thing to say as they both smiled at each other and left.

After several more parties where I was actually in town and could attend (Thanks, Amy), things got crazier and crazier as we both started meeting more people. So they tried to evict me, but to no avail. My neighbor took an overseas assignment shortly thereafter.

Our porn star friend became so well-known that she parlayed her notoriety to become a well-known Japanese businesswoman. She speaks English with a slight hint of a New York accent.

A Massage Like No Other

*We were taken to a small room where they told us to
get completely naked and put on a helmet. I had never
needed a helmet for a massage before.*

Many of the other Americans and Europeans were in a
similar boat to mine in Tokyo. Very few people liked them
or interacted with them either. One day, one of my new
best friends, Ken (half-Japanese, half-American and always
looking for fun) told me about this stress-reducing massage/
bath place. He assured me it was not one of these sex places
disguised as a massage parlor. I decided to go anyway.

It was an "Onsen" and it was located in the heart of Tokyo.
The "onsen" is basically a Japanese public bath with natural hot
spring water. From a Japanese guidebook I found this quote:

*"The onsen plays an important role in Japanese culture,
providing (socially) institutionalized relief from the pressures
of the contemporary Japanese twelve-hour work ethic and a
chance for Japanese to break down the hierarchal nature of
society through the mutual nakedness of skinship."*

I don't think I've ever seen a sentence quite like that one and didn't even know skinship was a real word. I was also a bit nervous about the mutual nakedness part.

Ken and I met after one particularly stressful day of work and headed over by subway stuffed with seemingly 10 million Japanese also getting off from work. They actually have people on the subway platforms called pushers who insure that the maximum number of people are on any given subway car at any given time. Often it feels like there is not a single inch of room left, but they find a way to add about 10 more people to your car by shoving them in the back and launching them into you. It's quite the enjoyable way to begin and end a day.

After elbowing our way out of the crushed subway car, we began our 10-minute walk to the Onsen. We arrived at a department store and Ken said, "We're here." Since I couldn't imagine getting a bath/massage in the hardware section or the jewelry section, I had no idea what was going on. He instructed me to get on this special elevator next to the department store. I use the word elevator hesitantly as it really was more similar to a vertical MRI machine or a vertical coffin, as the cylinder looked like it was designed for one small Japanese person. Ken made us both squeeze in and two others joined us. I could barely breathe. My relaxing after-work experience was not going well.

Since we were on the ground floor, I assumed we were going up, but lo and behold our oasis of stress relief was actually on B-4. That meant we were heading below the basement, underground 4 levels. I felt like a coal miner going to work or a visitor to Hell as we slowly, claustrophobically descended.

I could see in the darkness Ken's twisted smile. Ken spoke fluent Japanese so at least I hoped things would be OK.

We finally arrived and three elderly Japanese ladies welcomed us with cups of relatively disgusting green tea. The ladies looked very pale as if they had lived underground at B-4 for the last 50 years. Perhaps they had.

After paying 15,000 yen (about $135, a seemingly high amount for skinship), the women led us to a changing room where we hung up our clothes and put on a Japanese yukata (cotton robe). Ken explained to me that there was a specific sequence of treatments and preparations we would encounter, some more pleasant than others.

We were taken to a small room where they told us to get completely naked and put on a helmet. I had never needed a helmet for a massage before. I started to question the ladies in English and then in what I believed was Japanese, but they just giggled at me. They escorted us to another room where they told us to hold onto the handles attached to the wall. I felt like I was about to be executed, and given the circumstances it didn't seem like a bad alternative.

Two different older women appeared in what can best be described as a fireman's outfit. The situation was getting so surreal I was now actually ready for the adventure, or so I thought. They brought out two giant, powerful hoses and began spraying us like we were cars going through a car wash. The force was incredible and we could barely hold on to our handles. My screams were not heard above the power of the water. Ken was taking it all in peacefully somehow. Finally after about two minutes (it seemed never-ending), the hoses were turned off and we were told to turn around and face them, as it was time for the front side to be hosed down. I was scared out of my mind. I didn't know whether to hold onto the handle with one hand and protect my "privates" with the other, or keep holding onto both handles and let my privates take on the raging power of the water.

I now understand why the helmet was necessary, as I chose the one-hand approach and could barely hold on for the next two minutes. I felt like my shoulder had been ripped out of its socket as well. Finally, the onslaught ceased and we were allowed to remove our helmets. I must admit some dirt was removed from my body in that process, along with three birthmarks it seemed.

They led us to the "cold tank" where one must sit for 3-5 minutes. It was like falling into a frozen pond up north if the ice had broken loose. I was too tired to scream anymore and I didn't know the Japanese phrase for "Please just shoot me now."

With teeth chattering, we were able to leave our penguin-like confines for the next stop on our tour, the hot sauna. After being nearly frostbitten, the sauna felt good, albeit really toasty. My heart had been through intense cold and then intense heat, which I assumed was medically safe. I was assured that it was safe for the Japanese, but they weren't quite sure for Americans. After about 10 minutes of heavy sweating we were led to the assembly line of matted tables. We were told to get up on the tables and lay quietly on our stomachs completely naked. Ken whispered to me that this might not be my favorite part. I had already had many "not favorite parts" so I was starting to get worried. In very fast Japanese, the woman asked me something about soft, medium or hard. Given that I was completely naked I assumed "hard" was the right answer but for a very different reason than she was asking, as it turned out.

With my eyes closed and teeth clenched (how relaxing!) the woman sprayed me with sudsy-like stuff from a container and began to scrub me as hard as she could with a bristled brush that people use to clean extremely grungy tile grout. She was trying to remove dead skin but given how raw my skin became I think she got a few epidermal levels deeper than necessary. She scrubbed every inch of my back, butt and legs. When she heard me giggle after she hit a few particular spots, she increased the pressure, which seemed physically impossible.

I was hosed off and yanked to where my back was flat down on the table. I tried to say, "Enough already, I'm ready to get back in the cylinder and onto a crowded subway," but I was too frozen in disbelief as to what was happening. Plus I clearly didn't know that phrase in Japanese. She started scrubbing my neck, then down to my shoulders, and then down to my chest with this porcupine-like tool which was quite painful. As she moved her way down to my stomach I became very concerned as to the next stop. As she got to my groin area she explained in really broken English that would cost extra, which I declined. She finished up with my legs, toes and the bottom of my feet and again hosed me down. I was now devoid of skin.

They rolled me off the table and told me to wait in the

corner with my yukata on. Every inch of my body screamed out. Ken said the best was yet to come, which wasn't hard to believe since every other experience there was full of its own level of pain. After about 10 minutes we were led into a private room of several more typical looking massage tables. Finally, some real relaxation I thought. As we were led in, Ken informed me that these masseuses were 75-year-old women who were blind but great with their hands and feet. I was so turned on I could barely control myself.

As I climbed onto the table, I just closed my eyes and thought of how I would get Ken back for this insanity, which brought some pleasant, evil thoughts to mind. As if from a Kung-Fu movie, the women almost leapt on the tables in perfect synchrony, landing right on our backs with their knees. The pain was like no other. They proceeded to massage (I guess that's the closest word) our backs with their knees and their toes for 30 minutes and removed knots in my back I never realized existed. They flipped us over and expertly maneuvered their fingers into nerve endings that needed to be touched—I guess. After about an hour of this I was too exhausted to get off the table. The blind lady maneuvered me off the table—I was glad she grabbed the right area to maneuver me as I had turned over and she obviously could not see that. Boy, did she have strong hands/arms. We were led to the final area where we could just soak in a nice, warm tub.

We got out of the tub, dried ourselves off, and painfully got back into our regular clothes. The inside of my brain felt full of water from the initial firewoman's hosing, my skin was raw from the scrubbing, and my throat was sore from screaming.

Our mutual nakedness experience was over. My skinship with Ken had reached new levels.

Ken and I entered the elevator cylinder alone and began our ascent to the world above. It felt roomier with all that extra skin removed. We walked slowly to the subway as our feet were beginning to blister from the scrubbing.

We got on the subway platform and seeing the crowded train decided to wait for the next one. Five seconds later we were launched by a pusher into the crowded train (so much for waiting) and were seemingly up in the air, bayoneted against three pointy umbrellas for the 15-minute trip home. I don't think I was ever so sad about a forecast for rain.

I found my couch and laid on it for the next two days watching Japanese TV that I could not understand a word of. I didn't even care. I was covered in some supposedly special blister-reducing salve (or so the Japanese pharmacist claimed it was in broken English when he sold it to me) from my toes to my ears and all spots in-between. Ken, in his perfect Japanese, had gone to a different pharmacy and somehow he was in much better shape than I was a few days later.

Ken and I had many great times together during my three years living in Japan, though the Tokyo Onsen was not a repeat trip. I returned to the U.S. in 1986 while Ken stayed, given his parents lived there. We stayed in touch over the years but unfortunately, Ken passed away in 2001 from cancer. I'm sure Ken is watching over his Japan buddies from above and is probably the cleanest guy in Heaven.

I've had a lot of massages since in the U.S., and have never been asked to put on a helmet again.

Fertility and the Yakuza

Trying to decide between dying via poison and being rude to a yakuza that had taken us under his wing, we decided to eat the fish.

After checking Google, Amazon.com, and a few other Internet sites, I found that no one had ever used the above chapter title before, which really highlights how weird a time I had in Japan one particular weekend.

There are different festivals in some part of Japan almost every weekend. Some are serious tributes, some are pure fun, and one in particular was one my gaijin (foreigners) group just had to attend for the pure insanity of it all. We were not disappointed.

Held every April 15th (way more fun than U.S. tax day) at Wakamiya Hachimangu Shrine in Kawasaki, the Kanamara Matsuri festival is about as wild as they get. I knew it was going to be a strange day when my buddies of about five men and five women approached the tiny ticket booth to enter the Fertility Festival. My roommate Amy was with me along with good friends Emmett, Dick, Blair, Val and Audrey, to name a few.

I was first in line of my group and paid 1,000 yen ($7.00) to enter. So far so good. I was then asked in Japanese by the oldest woman I had ever seen, "Chinpo" or "Manko?" After quickly consulting my Japanese pocket dictionary, I learned these words referred to the male and female genitalia. I decided to answer with "Chinpo," which caused a weird smile to appear on the old woman's face. I started to turn bright red. She then asked in very broken English using her hands spread apart "small, medium or large?" Redness continued to take over my face, neck, and ears.

She had spread her hands out about three feet for the large so I decided to say "medium," which had her chuckling loudly, covering her mouth in pure glee. I thought I was going to be asked next to drop my pants for an inspection, and that definitely concerned me. The medium was still a foot and half long, so clearly I was very much busted.

For this festival, people of all ages march in a parade in which they attach a gigantic rubber chinpo (or manko) on their heads. These are available in a variety of sizes, hence the questions from the old lady. My friend Emmett was handed a large one but his was defective and kept deflating, so having a shriveled large one on top of his head did little in his quest to meet new people. When he finally did get it re-inflated it would go straight up for about a foot and then make a sharp right turn for the other two feet. The moral I learned was that it's not always good to have a large one.

As our group marched around for two hours with rubberized chinpos and mankos on our heads while drinking sake, the world became a lot clearer and cheerier. I am thinking about starting this parade in Boca Raton, but I'm not sure how it will go over. I asked Emmett if he would attend but he said he is still bothered by his first experience.

Boarding the bus back home for Tokyo, I must admit we did get more than a few stares from people. It must have been the Hawaiian shirts we were wearing. Except for my neck hurting for a week (it's heavy to carry a medium-sized rubber chinpo on your head for two hours if you have not tried it before), it was one heck of a weird day that I mistakenly thought was nearing its end.

When my roommate Amy and I got home that night (she had looked quite attractive with her orange rubber manko on her head), there was a message on our answering machine from one of the highest-level guys in the Japanese yakuza. Since the yakuza is the equivalent of the Mafia one might normally be extraordinarily alarmed. At first I wasn't sure if we had broken some super religious custom at the Fertility Festival. It turns out he was one of Amy's more "interesting" friends (she had a number) who wanted to come over and party. We were pretty burnt out from the day but you don't say "no" too often to the yakuza. We removed our rubber headgear in advance and hid them outside on the balcony.

He had visited our apartment many times in the prior six months along with some of his friends (all tattooed, impeccably dressed, and all with half of their left finger cut off as part of their initiation ritual). They were some of the nicest, kindest, most generous (at least to us) people we had ever met. Often our friend would take us out to the top restaurants in Japan that had three-hour waits, and somehow we would get seated immediately at the best table. A bill never arrived for any of the meals. He took us to the hottest clubs in Japan and again we were whisked to the VIP champagne rooms instantly, always with no bill at the end. We went to places that weren't even on the map where wining, dining and entertainment were beyond five stars. It was quite the phenomenal six months.

That night we were sitting around drinking some special sake flown in from a far-off Japanese island by our friend, when he announced his surprise that we would be dining on fugu tonight. Fugu is a delicious fish if prepared by a fugu-licensed chef. It is a delicious fish that kills people due to its internal poisons if not properly prepared by an expert. Our friend had zero experience preparing fugu (or any kind of fish), but decided that he was drunk enough to learn that night and was kind enough to have Amy and me try the first few bites. Trying to decide between dying via poison and being rude to a yakuza that had taken us under his wing, we decided to eat the fish.

I let Amy go first (the gentleman that I am) and she did not have any immediate purplish color on her skin or any unusual gagging noises. I stalled for as long as I could just in case it was a slow-acting poison. My turn was due and with my chopsticks wiggling like I had an uncontrollable nerve disorder, I took a small, careful bite. As soon as it was in my mouth, my life partially flashed in front of me (including the Fertility Festival) but all I could say was "Tastes like chicken," which made them laugh. As it turns out, we got very lucky and did not get sick or die, though the terror certainly caused a few gray hairs.

As we finished dessert, he told me he wanted to talk to me alone outside. Already that day, I had worn a giant rubber chinpo on my head, I had eaten a fish that kills hundreds per year and now one of the top guys in the Japanese yakuza wanted to talk to me outside on my seventh story balcony. I had already been told a few days prior that my three-year stint in Japan would be over in about three months and was now wondering if I grabbed my medium-sized rubber chinpo, whether I could land on it seven stories down and still survive. I found myself wishing I had purchased the large. I also wondered what the newspaper picture of me splattered on the ground with my rubber toy would look like to my friends, family and bosses at Motorola.

When we got outside on the balcony, he put his arms around my shoulder and went through a lengthy list of the experiences we had shared (and the money I never laid out). Shaking my head up and down in agreement (my neck still hurting from the Fertility Festival), I wasn't exactly sure where the conversation was going.

He pointed out that he (and his crew/under lords) had been everywhere in Japan and he meant everywhere from the top restaurants to the fanciest geisha houses. He said there was one place he had never been and he saw me as his ticket in. He wanted this one favor before I left Japan. I tried to imagine how I could help him in Japan, how much it would cost me, and how much trouble I would wind up in, but I still could not fathom any list of possibilities. I also knew that I couldn't say no.

Recognizing my befuddlement and my growing fear, not to mention his concern that I was squeezing my chinpo to the point it almost popped (the rubber one), he simply said "I want full access for one day to the Tokyo American Club." The American Club is a fancy country club in the heart of Tokyo that's so expensive only expatriates working for top U.S. companies (membership paid by the companies) were allowed in, along with their blue-blood guests. Motorola has since changed their policy, per below I would have to guess.

My few American bosses and their wives went regularly along with the top American families from other companies along with their children. I went once in awhile for brunch. As far as I knew, there hadn't been too many yakuza in their hot tub before. Since I didn't die from the fugu and I wanted to get off the balcony quickly (via the door), I said "Of course."

The following morning our friend and five of his under lords all showed up at my apartment around 10:00. We took two of his fleet of expensive European cars with black-tinted windows down to the American Club and I showed my Club card to the guy at the front gate along with my guest passes. For an 80-year old security guard used to waving in the president of a U.S. hi-tech company, his wife and their children (Buffy and Dexter), he was quite overwhelmed to see six people with no left finger, tattoos all over their bodies, standing there in Speedos. I made my way in with a hat and sunglasses, trying to protect my identity. The yakuza guys thought they had reached Nirvana. They threw their towels and bags aside and jumped into the heated swimming pool as if they were young kids again, splashing all around. The buzz among the regulars was stunningly loud as no one could figure out how they got in. They got out of the pool, ordered cheeseburgers and fries, chocolate malts, etc. and thought they were fitting in as normal Americans. Of course, I ran into my boss, who was completely shocked and appalled (guess I shouldn't have worn my Motorola logo hat) though his kids thought it was kind of cool.

After about three hours of frolicking, the boys had had their fun and we got up to leave. We took the convoy back to the apartment and drank some sake and beer, and they laughed and laughed about their day. They called a number of their friends jealously telling them about their big day. They liked me so much that I was afraid they might offer me an honorary initiation, and my left finger began to shake.

The following weekend our friend called again and wondered if we could do it again for some of his other yakuza friends. I had already been expelled from the American Club (plus my boss had made me sit down with Human Resources and a counselor to see if I needed any help), so I asked if he could serve me some more of the poison fugu instead.

Branded on Mt. Fuji

I think at the very top of the mountain the Japanese
character that they give only to Americans means
"Idiot."

Near the end of my stay, I was told I should climb Mt.
Fuji, as it's something "everyone must do once." Mt. Fuji is a
13,500-foot mountain that takes about 6-8 hours to climb and
must be started at around 10:00 p.m. due to the heat in the
summer during the day and the goal of reaching the top as the
sun just begins to rise. I am not into heights, and I enjoy going
to bed around 10:00, so I can't say I was thrilled about the
thought of it. But since I was leaving in a couple of months, I
figured it couldn't kill me. Boy was I close to being wrong.

Our bus of about 75 people from Tokyo arrived at Mt.
Fuji at 9:30 p.m., joining what seemed like 100 other buses
of 75 people from all over Japan. I was with Amy, my friend
Emmett, and a few other friends. We all bought walking sticks
to help navigate and also because at each 1,000 foot level
there is a little old man with a branding iron that burns some
Japanese characters into your stick indicating your progress. I

think at the very top of the mountain the Japanese character that they give only to Americans means "Idiot."

As we prepared for our ascent, it was amazing to see 80-year-old women starting to head up, people on bikes trying to handle the narrow rocky paths, blind people with seeing eye dogs (you would really have to trust that dog), and a few Americans besides our crew. For the most part it was young Japanese people trying to have fun and escape the crowds of the big cities, only to find crowds on a faraway mountain. We all dipped into our dried sardine snacks to get some energy and drank some lukewarm green tea.

I was hoping for some very wide paths with no ledges that one could possibly fall off of. For much of the beginning it was like that and I grew cocky that this wasn't too bad. As midnight approached and weariness began to sink in, the path became more and more narrow and I could see huge drop-offs to my left. It was a good place for an American to be accidentally pushed off to never-never land.

People rushed past us, which was pretty hard given the narrow space. We kept on pushing and pushing away up steeper and steeper slopes, some of which definitely bordered on treacherous, and at higher altitudes where breathing was harder. I was no longer tired as my adrenaline had kicked in as I thought the "end was near," and not meaning the "end of the trail." We were getting our branding iron burns along the way, which were cute but did not relieve the burning in my thighs.

As we got close to sunrise we could actually see the peak of the mountain, which was actually exciting. We were only a few hundred yards away. I soon learned that at 13,000 feet there is so little oxygen that it took only a few steps to completely collapse before resting, taking a few steps and collapsing again. The last 100 yards took about 30 minutes and it was entirely pain-filled. If I had planned on staying in Japan longer, Amy would have certainly received her eviction notice from my apartment. After seven hours of torture, I crawled to the top of the peak where Amy, Emmett and the others were there with a camera taking a picture of me. They barely recognized me as the color of my skin had a greenish tint to it. After 30 minutes of lying down, I was able to get my bearings and saw the most beautiful sunrise ever as we were above the clouds.

I asked Amy how the busses were going to get up to the top to get us down. She laughed and said that the hike was only half-over. I couldn't believe it. I ate some more dried sardines and began the slide down the back of the mountain. This route had us go through thick gravelly-like lava, which felt like we were running in quicksand. When we were halfway down the mountain it started getting really hot, but we kept on going all the way to the bottom. I was exhausted to say the least. I'm not sure if I felt worse physically or mentally that the club of 80-year-old women was flying by us in unison barely breaking a sweat.

When we got back on the bus my friends considered taking me to the hospital instead, and I slept the whole way back to Tokyo. They peeled me off my seat two hours later and we took a cab back to my apartment. There would be no parties tonight. I passed out in bed in my walking gear, holding my stick with all the branded characters next to me. I woke up the next morning sore all over. Amy asked me what I thought and I said, "I can understand why people only do this once."

I must admit the pictures my friends gave me of my final crawl to the peak were classics (very funny in retrospect) and my pictures of the sunrise were spectacular. As time went on, I began to be very thankful that I had completed such an intense adventure with such good friends. I still have that old stick in my house but must admit I haven't had a dried sardine since.

4. The Opposite Sex

THERE'S THIS FAMOUS BOOK called "Men are from Mars, Women are from Venus." From my experience those planets are too close together to represent reality. Blind dating, regular (if there is such a word) dating, chance encounters, marriage . . . which woman made all the rules?

Blind Dating Hell

I'm looking for the future mother of my children, not an all-nighter of wild sex with a stunningly beautiful girl.

When I was in my early thirties, I decided I was ready to settle down, get married, have kids, and get some goldfish. The problem was that I was either working, or lying in my recliner watching sports and not really putting myself in a position to meet women. Dating people from work was a bit dangerous and too public, so I was left with the "outside of work" opportunities.

I decided to start off with the bar scene as I figured I had a far better chance with drunk women who were desperate to meet men than with sober women who could see my stories coming from a mile away.

For the first month, I hit the Friday happy hours from 5:00–8:00 p.m. The next month I tried the mid-shift from 10:00 p.m. to midnight—going home to take a nap first after work. In the third month I tried the really late shift from 1:00–4:00 a.m. —going home and getting almost a full night's sleep first. After three long months, I wound up with lots of hangovers, lots of loser male friends trolling the same places, and no women that I really hit it off with.

The next month I tried some Single Mingles (groups of singles getting together for a fee at a given location), which was a really embarrassing group of people. They seemed even more desperate than I was (which was saying a lot). Most of the men had such incredible comb-overs that I would often be caught just looking at their heads, which wasn't a good starting place to chat up a woman. The women had seemingly all been divorced a few times and their plastic surgery was insanely obvious (not that I'm knocking well-done plastic surgery).

I finally decided that I couldn't succeed by myself and that I needed help from friends. Thus began my journey to "blind date hell." At first I thought it was a great idea. It seemed logical that someone who knew me well and knew someone else well should be able to figure out if the two of us would be a good match.

The first person I spoke to about this was my female hairdresser of five years, who knew a lot of women. She knew I was obsessed with sports so she thought long and hard, and by my following haircut appointment she had decided that Paddy O'Halloran was perfect for me. In fact, she had already spoken to Paddy, who was fine with me calling her. I was betting that she wouldn't meet my mother's Jewish criteria given her last name, but I was not letting that stand in my way if she was really "the one".

I was pretty excited, called her, had a pleasant, quick chat and agreed to meet her for a drink in one of the popular bars for happy hour the following Friday night at 7:00. I got to the bar early and had two drinks, as I was definitely a bit nervous about meeting Paddy. I saw some of my loser male bar friends and bragged that while they would be trolling and failing tonight, I was actually about to have a real date which would be headed for lifelong bliss. Maybe it was actually four drinks that I had, given that I was already thinking of lifelong bliss with a girl I had never laid eyes on.

I had no idea what this girl looked like, but she had told me she'd be wearing a blue top and gray pants. I kept anxiously watching the front door of the bar but no one appeared. I couldn't believe that I might be getting stood up and started hearing grief from my friends. They, on the other hand, looked frightful trying their raps out on unsuspecting single women. I wondered if I looked the same on my typical night out.

About 7:20 p.m., in walked a woman with a blue top and gray pants who I hesitantly waved over to my booth. She was 5'2, 175 pounds, with massive arms, shoulders and thighs. Paddy shook my hand and my fingers were almost crushed. I was happy that she didn't try to hug me hello. Paddy not only loved watching sports on TV (one of my top criteria), she also played catcher for Tommy's Irish Tavern girl's softball team. It was then that I noticed the creases on her forehead and cheeks from where her catcher's facemask had been from recent days. It was not a pretty sight. I quickly looked down at her legs to see if her shin guards were still on.

I asked her if she would like a glass of white wine but she said she wanted a pitcher of beer and three tequila shots for herself. The beer and tequila was all consumed by the time I got back from the bathroom where I was trying to figure out an escape plan. My dream of lifelong bliss with Paddy was over in less than 10 seconds. I silently cursed my hairdresser.

After about 30 minutes of small talk (and more shots of tequila for Paddy), I told her that while I was really enjoying the evening (despite looking at my watch every 2-3 minutes), I needed to leave because I had promised to help out with the Bingo game that night at the "Assisted Living Home for Jewish Men who Whine." (This was a place most Jewish men easily qualified to get in.) She was happy about my charitable work, wished me well and hoped I could attend her softball game in the near future. I told her I might try, but word quickly got back to my hairdresser from both of us that neither mothers needed to go out and buy their dresses quite yet, though I did wonder how Paddy's mother might look in a pretty chest protector.

Since my female-friend route failed, I figured my buddy Jimmy might be better since he and I hung out a lot and he knew a lot of women. He told me to give his Jewish friend Devorah Ginsberg a call, which I did. She also sounded great on the phone but after my nice phone encounter with Paddy, I didn't trust the phone anymore for any indications. I also learned not to meet a blind date in a place where I knew people. I agreed to meet Devorah in a nice restaurant/bar a bit off the beaten path.

The following Friday I was ready to try it again and I put on my lucky shirt and pants. Actually, they were new clothes as I realized I had no lucky shirts, pants, shoes, socks, or anything else.

At the bar I heard a voice behind me say, "Arnie, is that you?" I turned around and was shocked to see this beautiful brunette with long hair and a great figure. I was so surprised, I squealed in an embarrassing, pre-puberty voice, "Devorah, is that you?" It was, and visions of little Goldbergs running around our new home and going to temple danced in my brain. My mother was going to be shocked that I was actually going to be dating, and then of course marrying, a Jewish girl.

We had some drinks and a light dinner, and everything was going great. We talked and talked and talked. As midnight approached, I cautiously asked, with quite the stutter, if she would like to come back to my place. Despite the drool dripping down my chin, Devorah agreed to follow me in her car back to my place. I drove very slowly as I didn't want to have her get lost. For some reason, several women in the past had made very sharp right turns immediately after I made my last left turn onto my street.

We got to my driveway, where I fumbled around for my house keys as my hands were shaking in anticipation. Devorah grabbed my arm and said she was so happy to meet me.

I turned on the stereo, kept the lights low, and actually lit a candle (unfortunately the only one I had was a Jewish yahrzeit memorial candle). As I began to snuggle up to Devorah, and started to think of our future life together and how appreciative

I was of Jimmy finding me the perfect date, she whispered in my ear, "When will you be paying me my $200?"

I sat up, almost knocked over the yahrzeit candle, and in stunned amazement I asked what she was talking about. She told me she was a "working girl" whose real name was Maria Hernandez not Devorah Ginsberg, and that Jimmy had thought I would appreciate her. I asked her to leave. I said something along the lines of:

"I'm looking for the future mother of my children, not an all-nighter of wild sex with a stunningly beautiful girl." As the words were coming out of my mouth (and I started replaying in my head what I had just said), I quickly checked my wallet and unfortunately only had $50 on me. I wasn't sure how much that would get me, so I escorted her out the door. As she pulled away in her car, I was disappointed she didn't see me in her rear view mirror jumping up and down waving my credit card. I had come to my senses and decided that one night wouldn't be so bad. My 85-year-old neighbor, Sophie Schwartz who was walking her toy poodle, looked at me very strangely.

I decided to give up the blind dating approach as I was too overwhelmed by my experience with "Paddy the catcher" and "Devorah/Maria the call-girl." I also set my buddy Jimmy up with this great girl named Paddy on a blind date. Jimmy and I no longer speak.

20,000 Women in Bed

At the same time that I was pleading for her to stop, her naked parents entered the sauna. Talk about a mood killer.

After months of unsuccessful blind dating, I had given up hope of meeting someone who would actually want to marry me and vice versa. Deep down I knew, the "vice versa" might not be the hardest part of that sentence. I was in my mid-30's and figured lying around in my underwear watching football on Saturdays and Sundays eating chips, and drinking beer wasn't the worst thing after all. But I had decided that I needed to get married since I couldn't take any more weird dating experiences.

I had recently returned from an overseas trip visiting my Finnish girlfriend in her home country. I had met her in South Florida about six months before and I was on a business trip in Scandinavia. I arrived in Helsinki airport on a Friday evening and was greeted by my girlfriend and her parents, two people who looked very much like Mr. and Mrs. Claus. We drove for hours in a driving snowstorm to a tiny village.

They lived in a small house in the middle of a forest and it was quite picturesque.

After a little small talk (the parents did not speak much English and I zero Finnish), we sat down to eat reindeer. I had sad thoughts about poor Rudolph but managed to get a few bites in.

After dinner, the father stood up and said to me in a loud, deep voice, "Get naked!" I thought I heard the tune from *Deliverance* in the background for a moment. My girlfriend quickly explained that it was a special invitation to enjoy the wonderful sauna in their backyard. Not wanting to be left stranded in the middle of nowhere, I decided to follow his instructions. My girlfriend and I, in heavy robes, quickly marched through the snow path to the sauna about 50 feet from the house. It was a beautiful sauna and the temperature was great, especially compared to the freezing temperature outside.

As the sweat starting pouring off, two really bad things happened almost simultaneously. First, my girlfriend picked up a bunch of twigs wrapped together (called a vihta in Finnish) and proceeded to whack me with them from head to toe. This custom is supposed to help stimulate circulation and get the dirt in one's pores to come to the surface. It hurt like hell! At the same time that I was pleading for her to stop, her naked parents entered the sauna. Talk about a mood killer. They laughed and laughed at me, and I was too stunned to say anything.

My girlfriend asked if I would like to leave the sauna, and I was only too happy to leave. As we started heading back to the house, she told me that we needed to take a different path. Just wanting to take my bleeding skin anywhere quickly, I agreed but soon found myself at the foot of an icy lake. My girlfriend took off her heavy robe and proceeded to jump into the frigid water. Through chattering teeth, she told me that this was part of the custom and that I better get in. There was no way I was getting in. However, after a few minutes I spotted Mr. and Mrs. Claus rumbling naked in my direction (a very bad visual for sure), so I decided to take the plunge. It was beyond cold and I literally thought I had turned into a human popsicle. I got out as fast as I could and put my robe back on.

After returning to the U.S., I decided that it was probably time to find an American wife. I still had that blood-stained vihta as a reminder.

It was a few days before New Year's and I just couldn't imagine doing another Matzoh Ball or Jew Brew where all the single Jews get together at a club, get drunk, and make a wish at midnight. (Ladies, there are only so many doctors to go around!) One of my bachelor buddies, Stuart, said that a friend of his was having a party and wanted to know if I wanted to go along with him and a couple of the other "disease groupies." For those who do not know what a disease groupie is, in Boca Raton there are charity groups for every disease known to mankind. Some money is actually raised, but it's really an excuse to have a monthly party at some restaurant. At one point I was a member of both the Cancer and Heart Disease organizations which all the singles seemed to be in, but then wondered if I could meet someone more exotic elsewhere so I signed up for Leprosy and then Elephantitis. (It was weird seeing really heavy Boca women with thick legs at the Elephantitis outings, but that's just a strange aside.)

Six guys met at Stuart's house around 8:00 on New Year's Eve and drank a little, then drove to a local bar (to drink a wee bit more) packed like sardines in a Honda Civic that holds five people at best. One of us asked where we'd fit a woman if one of us picked up someone, then we all realized that — like all nights — we'd be coming back with the same group we left with.

We met my best friend, Carol, at the bar with some of her girlfriends and we headed over to the party. There were about 20 people gathered, munching on food and drinking away. It was, after all, New Year's Eve, and there's nothing like getting on the road around 12:30 a.m. with lots of other drunken people.

I saw one person that I knew, Jake, who was on a date with this nice looking blond—let's call her Karen (my wife's name coincidentally). I also saw talking to them, the largest human I had ever seen. It was Wilt Chamberlain, the 7'2" basketball player who made his home in Boca Raton and had his own restaurant in town. Even at the age of 55, he looked like he had only 10% body fat (compared to my 60%, which might only appear to be 40% to an alcohol-induced woman). I was 5' 10' with my lifts. Wilt Chamberlain had just released his autobiography where he infamously (or famously) claimed he slept with 20,000 women. His average was about 1.5 women every day for 30-35 years. I had the same average numerator, just a way different denominator.

Jake was a good-looking guy who lifted weights for fun. I walked over (stumbling was probably a bit more accurate) to Jake and his date along with my friend Carol, and looked up into Wilt's face and introduced myself as someone very knowledgeable about his records. He rattled off things like his 100-point game, his 50-point game average for a season, etc.,until I slurred something about the 20,000 women. Somehow he must have had a better rap with women than I did (not difficult), so I was anxious to hear his pick-up lines. Given that we were in earshot of a number of women, he did not take kindly to my words. He picked me up by my shirt collar and carefully dumped me on the other side of the party. Jake looked shocked and his date laughed hysterically. Carol was left shaking her head at me, as she was apt to do over the years.

I gradually made my way back to Jake and his date, and kept on getting beers for Jake in the hopes that his bladder was not as big as his biceps so that I could steal some time alone with Karen. I finally got a few minutes alone to slur some suave lines (I thought they were suave) at her, though it didn't appear any of them were swaying her to come join me in the Honda Civic with five other guys or anything close to that.

At the end of the night and alone for about two minutes with her, I asked what her last name was so I could call her. She told me it was "Coleman like the lantern." Being the non-camper, I had absolutely no idea what she was talking about but promised I would track her down. I asked her if she was into "Leprosy" but she looked at me with a very puzzled expression. She told me that I was just a typical Boca New Year's partier and would not even remember we met. I said goodbye to Jake and told him I knew a great girl named Linda he might be interested in that would be more his type than Karen. He also looked at me puzzled, especially since I never brought this up to him previously (and frankly there was no girl I knew named Linda). I waived goodbye to Wilt but he did not see me a full foot and four inches below him.

The next day I called all the "Lanterns" in the telephone book (I felt like the prince trying to find Cinderella) with no luck. I knew I couldn't call Jake and ask him for his date's phone number, since I was planning on trying to steal her away and that seemed rude enough. At least I would have to work for the number.

A few days later, I was at my friend's Stuart's house and we were hanging out in his garage shooting some pool when I noticed of all things a lantern—a "Coleman brand" lantern, and suddenly my synapses started firing on most cylinders and I remembered that I was supposed to track down Coleman—not Lantern. There were lots of Colemans in the Boca Raton telephone book and I started calling them all asking if they had ever met Wilt Chamberlain. Many of the husbands that answered the phone did not seem overly pleased by the question.

I finally tracked down Karen, who was shocked that I actually remembered her name. I told her I didn't feel right asking her out for a date since she was dating Jake, but asked if we could meet for a drink to discuss if we might one day marry and have children. She thought I was absolutely insane, made me explain that I did not have leprosy, and agreed to one drink.

I guess she thought I was funny, or liked out-of-shape guys, or thought Jewish guys had money, but lo and behold I was in and Jake was out over the next month. Karen and I got married about 18 months later. Neither Jake nor Wilt made it to the wedding.

I Love You – Now Change!

I was walking around waving to people and some actually waved back. I was feeling the love—I was feeling the beginning of my new being. My wife was going to see a new me.

I'm not sure what the hardest year of one's life is. Perhaps it's the first year of your life. Perhaps it's the first year of elementary school, or perhaps it's the first year of high school when no girls will go out with a male freshman. Or perhaps it's the senior year of high school when you realize the girls still won't go out with you. I'm not necessarily speaking of my own high school experience but...

In looking back, the most exciting but most challenging year was my first year of marriage. I'm sure my wife would say it was also her most difficult one since she is much easier to deal with than I am, as I've been told by most everyone who meets us.

You think it's going to be relatively easy since you've dated for a couple of years and know the person very well. You obviously love the person, so you figure how hard can it be living side by side virtually 24/7, 365 days a year for 50 years, but who's counting at that point? The wedding is full of complete joy and you think of all the perfect days ahead.

The honeymoon in a romantic resort went great and the first few months of living under the same roof as Mr. and Mrs. Goldberg was fantastic. My shikse wife had a little trouble being called "Goldberg" as most church-going women might, but over time it became more natural. I had a little trouble watching the Lifetime channel, but I quickly learned when I should cry as sincerely as I could fake it. I don't think she ever faked anything, but that's probably a different book.

All was going well until that fateful trip to Orlando to the theme parks. That might be hard to believe since the parks are full of magic, thrills and adventure. The downfall began with the fact that the parks were actually full of people more than anything else.

My wife is at the head of the category of "friendliest humans," while I am more in the category of "want more potato chips" to my buddy in my living room watching football. Ever since I was in high school (maybe due to the lack of distraction of going out with women), I always had a small group of really good friends and couldn't be bothered with the peripheral small talk necessary to deal with lots of other people. My wife, on the other hand, gets holiday cards from the garbage men, shares recipes with the mail lady, and likes going to the grocery store to talk to the cashiers.

In Orlando, you spend a countless amount of time standing on lines among thousands of people. There are those from England; the black socks and shoes give them away long before your hear their accent. There are people from obscure cities in the Midwest where many look like they did not get the memo about the obesity epidemic sweeping the country. You think you've seen the record for eating doughnuts at 7:00 a.m. one day in your hotel, but then it's broken the next. Where is Guinness when you need those record keepers? And stereotypes aside, you've got to admit Japanese people certainly take a lot of pictures. It is a bit embarrassing when you see once-proud Japanese titans of business being told to "run over there as we've just got to get a picture of Goofy and Mickey together."

The one true thing about all these people is that the Goldbergs will never, ever see any of them again (I can only hope). My wife thinks we are the two-person force of the freakin' Florida chapter of the United Nations or the volunteer army of the theme parks, and therefore by sworn duty we must welcome all visitors to our state's parks. I remind her that we just paid hundreds of dollars for a four-day pass, so it's not like it's "our" back yard with its zero charge for admission. She counters by saying that we're on these long lines anyway and do I really want to talk to her for eight hours straight? I know it's a trick question and I watch her go into her Mother Theresa role. I'm not sure why she thought people with hard-to-understand accents would understand her better if she spoke really, really loudly but she did and they either didn't know how to say "pipe down ye wonderful volunteer" or were just in shock.

During the first three days of our four-day extravaganza, my wife must have talked to over 100 people from all over the world. I had talked to the burger guy, the slushy girl, and the wheelchair vendor (my feet were killing me).

I was looking forward to the fourth day since we were going to a water park where you snorkel all day and get to interact with dolphins. I figured how much talking could there be underwater? We were checking out of the hotel and in the long checkout line, my wife managed to add seven more people to her list. On the trolley to the water park another five were added, and I'm not sure if I should count the two-minute conversation with the ticket-taker at the park or not.

We had a long conversation the night before, and my wife was clearly disappointed with my lack of desire to meet new people. She said that this was a major issue to her and that to insure a long and happy marriage, this was one area that I really, really needed to work on.

I tried to argue that we would never see these people again, but she quickly pointed out that we had been living in our neighborhood for eight months and I didn't even know our neighbors' names yet. Point taken. I promised her that I would try harder and that today would be the first day of my new being. I was not off to a good start that morning, as I wasn't a morning person with new people (or afternoon or evening). Maybe later in the day I would warm up to this new "friendly to strangers" thing.

The theme park was great though the water was quite cold. I guess keeping the fish alive was important. All the humans got full-body wetsuits as part of the admission process. I had never been in a wetsuit before and was amazed at just how snug they are. The nice girl behind the counter (not in a wetsuit) explained that the suit will feel bigger in the water and that people feel warmer, the snugger the fit. I bought that concept.

I was able to wriggle into the suit with great difficulty, though my wife had to "zip me up in the back" as there was no way to reach the full-length back zipper. It was a perfect day. We got to see giant stingrays, beautiful angel fish, and schools and schools of other fish in the reef. We were also underwater for most of the morning so I wasn't really forced to talk to anyone. We finished our morning snorkel and had a pretty decent lunch, topped off by the fact that the water park was owned by a major brewery so you could drink as much free beer as you wanted. It was great—they had beers that I had never seen before from all over the U.S. The sun was out, and the beer tasted great. And for free, who wouldn't take unnecessary, gluttonous advantage of the beer?

I was smiling and thinking that maybe I would actually consider talking to some strangers since everyone seemed pretty sloshed after lunch. I was walking around waving to people and some actually waved back. I was feeling the love—I was feeling the beginning of my new being. My wife was going to see a new me.

I told my wife that I needed to head to the main changing area to go the bathroom. She had just virtually tackled some lovely people from Poland and was in full "Welcome to America" mode.

I happily waddled down to the locker room in my snug

suit feeling good about the day. I headed to the urinal area and tried to undo my back zipper. I was not double-jointed, was quite buzzed, and had no shot. Too late, I realized that drinking lots of beer while locked into a full-length wetsuit was not ideal for trips to the little boy's room.

I laid down and tried to wriggle out of the wetsuit and looked like a fish just reeled onto the deck of a fishing boat. I next tried to lower the zipper by moving my back against the hanger you hang your bathing suit on, and I almost wound up hanging up my wetsuit and me in it on the hanger. Time was running out and I was low on options.

In walked four burly guys to go the bathroom; perhaps I would be rescued. Thinking of the double bonus of being a friendly member of society along with Mother Karen, and more importantly of actually being able to go the bathroom, I approached these giant Europeans and loudly said (thought maybe my wife was right about the necessity to speak loudly): "If you pull down my zipper, I will gladly pull down all of yours".

Since they had not yet tried to go the bathroom and were not yet aware of the pending doom, their reaction to my question was not a good one. They were offended, outraged and embarrassed, and one guy hit me so hard in the stomach that I thought his fist came through the other side. Another guy grabbed me near the neck and flung me around (actually loosening up the zipper) and I wasn't sure what to do next. I decided to crumple into a ball, which was quite easy and natural at that point. The four guys left cursing at me and muttering something like *"Queer Eye for the Straight Guy."*

Lying on the floor, I was somehow able to get the zipper on top of the floor drain (what a convenient place to land) and get it down far enough that I could slip out of my wetsuit and hobble over to the urinal. My wife was surprised to see me fully dressed since there was still a half-day left to go. I told her I had a bad stomach ache—must've been something I ate at lunch.

Fourteen years later, my wife is still incredibly friendly to all. She's president of our Neighborhood Welcome Committee and also president of the school's PTA. I think she sneaks out on weekends to go to the airport to welcome visitors. I, on the other hand, did not really ever recover from my water park attempt to interact with strangers. I have a few close friends that I watch TV with and go to the movies with. I do not snorkel or scuba dive with them or anyone. I think one of my neighbors is named Susan or Sally or something with an "S."

I tried a few of the many "suggestions" my wife had for me in that first year, and most of the time the cap of the toothpaste does make it back on, and most of the time the toilet seat is left down. However, when I fall below her current, low expectations of me (which is quite often), I remind her that she fell in love with the person she married—not some person she wants me to become. She wonders how my young sons continue to mature year after year, but her husband has somehow reached the "neutral" point of changing. She asks if all men stop maturing at 22 or 32 or 42. I tell her that I'm just glad I haven't started going in reverse yet.

The Other Woman

It's never good when another woman enters into your marriage.

As difficult as it is to adjust to being married, nothing compares to the challenges that come with becoming parents for the first time. Some of the unmistakable signs that you're a brand-new parent are:

1) You think the spit-up rag draping over your wife's shoulder is surgically implanted;

2) You've reached the point where dinner variety means different shapes of chicken nuggets; and

3) You haven't been out to the movies in so long that you're shocked at the ticket prices when someone tells you.

In Boca, there seems to be help for such challenging times. Many new parents in South Florida have their parents living down here, so grandma and grandpa are a big help in terms of advice, dropping off the kids for some "free" adult time, etc. Other new parents hire live-in nannies, realizing from the very beginning that they may not have a clue and could use some extra hands.

My wife and I decided to skip the nanny approach since it seemed like we could handle it and we wanted to make sure we were the two faces our kids saw regularly. That logic was before we had our first child.

With "2 on 1" coverage after our first son was born, we managed pretty well and got through the initial challenges.

When we had our second son a few years later, we realized that having two was going to be more than twice as hard. After about a year of stress, we decided to follow in the footsteps of a number of our neighbors and started considering the nanny option.

We had no idea what age the nanny should be, what nationality/country she should be from, or what experience level she should have. We asked around and found a lot of different opinions.

Finally, one of our neighbors told us that their young nanny (she called her an au pair) from Denmark had a 17-year-old friend, Marianne, from her home town who would be interested in coming for six months. We thought this was a good amount of time to be a reasonable test for both sides. We were also pleased that the reference came from such a solid source, since our neighbor's nanny was great with their kids, great helping out with the house, and really mature for her age.

Marianne was getting done with high school in a few weeks and she really wanted to begin right after that, so we didn't have a lot of time to decide. We exchanged a couple of emails and had one phone call with her and her family. Marianne sounded great, and even though she had never been a nanny before, she said she had been a babysitter for a number of years. Karen and I decided to go for it, and both sides were thrilled when Marianne accepted.

A few weeks later, the big day arrived and we were going to meet Marianne at the airport. Our whole family arrived at the international terminal early, not knowing how long the customs process might be. We had a big sign with our name on it since we had no idea what Marianne looked like and vice versa. Marianne's friend, our neighbor's nanny, was a nice girl who happened to be relatively short and a bit overweight.

As people entered the arrival area, we strained our necks to catch glimpses and raise our sign even more prominently. When we saw a few young women I would pounce on them excitedly with "Goldberg? Goldberg? Goldberg?" They scurried away none too pleased with their welcome to America.

Finally we saw this somewhat shy, homely-looking girl who was very confused. My wife slowly approached her without the giant poster board sign waving furiously, and calmly asked her if her name was Marianne. Sadly, the answer was no and we became concerned that our savior had backed out. The group of people coming into the arrival area had begun to thin appreciably.

A few businessmen entered the area, and an 85-year-old Chinese woman. I asked if she was here for "Goldberg" and she too scurried away. We were about to give up when we saw this tall, beautiful, scantily-clad girl looking around the arrival area. My sign was down around my ankles as I knew there was no way this almost-supermodel was a nanny. With my head down low having basically given up, I heard in a sexy accent, "Arnie? Karen?" I looked up and the supermodel was talking to us. Stunned and at full attention now, I wondered how she guessed our first names.

I look at my wife and she has already done the math. A beautiful 17-year-old woman who seems to enjoy very little clothing (even on a 10-hour cold plane ride) is about to live in her house for six months, along with her husband whose tongue is hanging below the three-foot high poster board sign. She's probably going to be out every night partying and meeting guys left and right. She's going to be too hung over and tired to help with the kids and the house.

I stammered "Marianne?" She responded with, "Hi, yes, I'm Marianne." I started doing my own math. A beautiful, 17-year-old girl is going to be relaxing in our pool in her thong bikini after a dedicated day of housework. She's going to want to stay around the house as much as possible because the Goldbergs are a lot of fun and can really help her learn about American culture. My young sons will love her. I will be there as much as possible to make her transition as easy as possible.

We got to the airport parking area, got in the car, and began the drive to Boca. My wife asked her about the plane ride, her family, her goals and aspirations. The only question I asked was whether she was dating anyone in Denmark. My wife glared at me, as it came out as if I was interested in pursuing a relationship with her, which was almost the furthest thing from my mind. Marianne said that she was currently single, but very interested in meeting an older American, someone around my age. I almost drove off the road, my wife's face turned very warm-looking, and my four-year-old giggled. I don't think he knew what was going on, but who knows.

We arrived at the house and I carried her bags to her room. My wife was close behind and fuming since I rarely (OK never) carry all of our bags into the house after a vacation. Marianne seemed very pleased with the service. At least two of us seemed to be happy.

It was about 3:00 on a hot sunny afternoon in June, and Marianne asked if it would be OK if she jumped in the pool since she'd had a long day of flying. Before Karen could tell her about the heavy chlorination that the pool service had done this morning and that it would be better to wait a day, I managed to blurt out way too quickly and excitedly, "that's a perfect idea."

Recognizing my misplaced excitement, Karen strongly suggested that we needed some things at the grocery store and sent me off with a longer list than I had ever seen before. I don't remember going through more than one red light, don't remember being told more than once to stop racing my shopping cart through the aisles, and certainly don't remember paying the cashier $20 to let me sneak onto the Express checkout line even though I had 32 items.

I rushed into the house, forgetfully leaving the milk to curdle in the car's trunk. I peered at the pool area looking like a puppy at the window hearing their owner's car door pull into the driveway. There she was—my new nanny—glistening in the rays of the sunshine. Like the young boy in *Animal House* who is so amazed that a beautiful cheerleader is catapulted through his bedroom window, I can only utter those same words, "Thank you God."

A strong tap on the shoulder broke my concentration and an insistent pointed finger (I believe it was the index finger) urged me to go back outside to retrieve our sons' food in the car. I started to wonder for an instant if this might not be such a perfect situation. Marianne asked for more suntan oil and I got over that fleeting thought that it might not work out.

After two hours in the sun, Marianne told us she was jet-lagged and exhausted from the sunning, so she decided to take a nap. Dinner came and went, and my wife made the whole meal without any help from our "sleeping beauty." Around 10:00 that evening, I heard some moaning from Marianne's room and I pounced off the couch, even though it was fourth and goal with one minute left in the football game. I'd been watching for three hours without moving. My wife was furious at me and I had to duck the avalanche of potato chips hoisted into the air from the bowl in my lap.

Marianne was simply stirring from her slumber. She told me she was going to shower now and I pointed her in the right direction. I stood outside the bathroom door for a minute or two or three to make sure she didn't need anything else. I may have waited longer but I heard this very loud "Arnie!" and saw my wife briskly walking toward me with potato chip crumbs between her toes. She said we needed to talk now. It wasn't really a talk or a discussion, since that usually means two people actually have words coming out. The soliloquy was well-delivered by my wife with very clear words and very clear purpose. If I didn't stop gawking and acting like a horny 16-year-old, I would have to go to permanent time-out.

Marianne got out of the shower, barely covered in towels.

I must have unintentionally erred by giving her two hand towels instead of a large bath towel. Silly me. My wife quickly addressed the situation with a robe and ushered me back to the television. At 11:00 it was time for bed, but Marianne was wide-awake, eager to explore Boca and go out for some coffee with her friend who is normally in bed by 10 p.m.

My wife's car was out of gas so I offered her the keys to my convertible. She was thrilled. My wife was less so.

Fast asleep at 2:00 a.m., I was barely disturbed by my wife's constant muttering and restless sleep. The phone rang shortly thereafter, never a good time to get a call. It was Marianne, and my car had disappeared. I was hoping "disappeared" in Danish meant something besides the English meaning. She went on to explain that she was in this bar, partying with some great new guys, and realized a bit too late perhaps, that the parking spot so convenient to the front door with the handicapped sign on it may not have been the best place to park.

I started calling the local car pounds and finally found my car. Karen told me to stay home with the kids and that she would straighten everything out. The first day was not going well, though Marianne did get a nice tan in only a couple of hours.

Marianne came in with her head bowed. She went to bed and woke up around noon, missing out on helping with the kids' morning meals and activities. It was a cloudy day so there would be no sunning for her today. I signed up for weather.com alerts so I could stay on top of potential sun outbreaks.

Over the course of the next few weeks, things got better as Marianne helped with the kids and helped Karen. She only went out four nights a week and she never took my car. By then, she owned three long robes, as my wife thought it would be a good idea to have extras, and the two one-piece bathing suits my wife bought her six months in advance of her birthday don't quite have the same appeal as the thong bikini, which was no longer displayed around my pool.

My kids loved her, which was the most important thing. Actually, in hindsight, I'm not sure if it was that important...

My guy friends and my brother insisted it was just so much fun visiting me almost daily for those six months to watch TV, play poker, and talk about life. As they would remind me, "if you can't please your friends, what is life about then?"

Marianne went back to Denmark and she has never been forgotten. Every time I see hand towels, I laugh at my "mistake."

Jump for Joy

She then pulled out two cables, dangling them in front of my face. I couldn't tell if she was trying to tell me to tie her up or vice versa, but the situation was getting weirder and weirder.

Did you ever have one of those days when nothing was going right and you just wanted the next day to come to get the bad luck over with?

My wife was out of town and I was in charge of our two boys, aged 11 and 8. It was a Friday morning and I was frantically trying to get my kids ready for school. I forgot to make their lunches the night before, so it was a mad scramble at 7:00 a.m. I looked for bread to make them sandwiches, but there was none left. I looked for pizza slices but they were gone as well. I decided to fill up their lunchboxes with old Halloween candy, as I wanted to get it out of the house and needed them to eat something at lunch. Not sure my wife would have made the same decision.

We ran to the bus stop and saw the taillights of the school bus pulling away. I would be driving them to school, a full 30 minutes further away from where I had to go to work. After getting them to school, I drove to work to find out that I had missed an important meeting that had begun at 8:00.

As the day wore on, it only got worse as a potential major client chose one of our competitors instead of us. I also had to spend two hours in a six by eight-foot conference room with a co-worker who had the flu. She kept apologizing in between nose blows. I told her to go home but she said she had run out of allowable sick days. I had a feeling I was going to be running out of mine shortly.

As I headed out from work that night, and approached my car in the parking lot, I saw a beautiful Latin woman standing by her car waving to me to come over. After I shook my head "no" to her question of "Habla español?" she said in broken English, "Can you jump on me?"

I thought of my lovely wife, my kids revved up from massive amounts of sugar intake, and the lousy day I had and said, "No, thank you, I just can't." She began to look sadder and sadder, and said more insistently, "Please, jump on me!"

I haven't read, though I have heard, that there is this section in the "gentleman" magazines where strangers meet in these happenstance ways (like in the middle of suburban parking lots) and romp off to extreme frolicking that is then detailed in a very graphic nature. I was about to find out if these outlandish stories were real or not.

Again, I tried to explain to her that I was happily married, I was going to miss dinner, and just couldn't "jump on her" even though she was one of the most beautiful women I had ever seen.

She then pulled out two cables, dangling them in front of my face. I couldn't tell if she was trying to tell me to tie her up or vice versa, but the situation was getting weirder and weirder. Finally she blurted out, "Battery dead—need jump." I quickly realized that this was not a *Penthouse* pre-story after all.

I regained my composure enough to say the little bit of Spanish I did know, "Yo comprendo." I didn't tell her I knew as much about cars as I did Spanish.

I got in my car and began the frantic search for the front hood release. In the 11 years that I've owned the same car, I never once had the urge to look at my engine. I found a small button with a picture of something popping open so I pressed on that and my trunk door slowly lifted. The girl could not tell why I was doing that. I stammered to her that I was just checking to see if any of my tools were in the trunk. (I own no tools).

I looked around some more and saw my gas cap button, various door and window lock buttons, and a whole bunch of other buttons in strange places. The girl came over and tried to figure out what was taking me so long. I finally found the hood unlock button and pressed it, turned around, and smiled at the girl. To my surprise, when I went to lift the hood, it was only raised about an eighth of an inch. I remembered that there might be another release mechanism and jammed my fingers into that little slot, from end to end of the hood, still trying to smile at the girl with confidence.

After about five agonizingly long minutes, I finally found the latch and pushed up the hood. My fingers were bloodied and crooked, but I tried to stay cool and look natural. Unfortunately, the hood wasn't staying there by itself and there was no "thing" (is it called a "hood holder?") to keep the hood up. I wasn't sure which cable to put on which battery thing or what part of the battery, but between us we guessed and prayed that we wouldn't electrocute ourselves.

With the cables all attached and me holding the hood up with one hand, I tried to stretch myself into my car at the same time to turn my car engine on. It was not a pretty sight. Just when I thought I might have a chance, the hood slipped and crushed the cables. She mumbled something in Spanish that didn't sound like a compliment.

Fortunately I started the engine, and she was able to start hers as well. We detached the cables without hurting ourselves. With a stern look, she said in broken English, "I'm glad I didn't need to use your tool."

When I pulled into my driveway, my wife asked why I was driving with my gas cap and trunk hatch both open. When I told her that I was helping someone jumpstart their car, I think she still wondered what that had to do with the trunk of the car, but she let me slide on that one because she was shocked that I was able to so easily (that's what I told her) help someone with their car troubles.

5. Ah, Sunny Florida!

I'VE LIVED IN SOUTH Florida for the better part of the last 25 years, although I had only planned on being here for two.

How could I leave? Sure we've got hurricanes and brutally hot weather, but early bird dinner specials are awesome!

There's No Place Like South Beach

We walked past one of the many happening Clubs for the beautiful people, well back behind the velvet ropes and soon realized that we had no chance of getting in. Young women with slinky dresses and giant breasts with no doggie bags seemed to be allowed in with ease.

We cross over the bridge from Miami airport to Miami Beach into a wonderful ocean paradise named South Beach, where young women who have made plastic surgeons wealthy are lying topless on the beach. Intersecting with that beauty, my 10 hair-thinning, belly-protruding college buddies descend on the beach, mouths agape, fully clothed. We looked a bit ridiculous but we don't care. We're turning 50, we're here for our big party, and it's a beautiful sunny day.

We weren't sure how our motley crew would fit into this jet-set environment, but we figured we could pull it off for at least a few days. Most of us act like we are 12 years old according to our wives, so the thought of 50 seemed a bit unreal. About once a year for the last 25 years, we have all gotten together with our wives to eat, drink and be stupid. Many of us have excelled beyond expectations, especially at the stupid part.

With literally thousands of students at college, it's always interesting to think how you just happened to meet those 10 people who have stayed lifelong friends. With my buddies, I always have to wonder if anyone else would have been insane enough to be friends with them or me.

We did all manage to graduate, some in four years, some in five, and a couple of us in six. I enjoyed studying in the library (that was the building with the ivy?) so much that I decided to extend my stay beyond the standard four years. At least that is what I told my parents. As we all left the friendly confines of the University of Rhode Island, we made sure we wouldn't lose touch so we set up annual get-togethers.

At our first rendezvous, we rented a giant house down on the New Jersey shore with 10 bedrooms and eight bathrooms. On the last evening, we christened our get-together as "Camp Laff-A-Lot" because that is pretty much what we did for 7 days and nights. We still go by that name and still spend plenty of time bursting out laughing.

I was given the task of travel agent for the 50th birthday party after we decided to have it in South Beach, relatively close to where I live.

In the old days at college, we could be at the Bon Vue bar in Narragansett, Rhode Island at 11:00 p.m. and by 2:00 a.m., be packed into a van driving 28 hours to Florida if someone had simply suggested the half-baked idea of "going to Fort Lauderdale soon for Spring Break."

Wow, how things have changed. People complained about only having five months notice to make plans; argued over whether we should stay at a cheap hotel two blocks off the main drag with no pool, a medium-priced place, or the most luxurious hotel with ocean-side massages priced for royalty; considered whether kids should come (not too much discussion on that one actually); and finally, whether wives should come (more discussion on that one).

Finally, I decided to take a secret ballot on the above, looked at the results, and chose what I wanted (only kidding if my friends are reading this). To everyone else reading this, isn't that what you would have done once you were given the role of travel agent?

Everyone flew in from different parts of the country on the first weekend in June (the hotel rates are much lower than mid-winter but you have to dodge the start of hurricane season and 95 degree days). We all met poolside at our beach hotel, and after a couple of "welcome" cocktails, the guys decided to head down to the ocean while the wives stayed at the pool.

As a kid, I used to love the feel and sound of the ocean waves, the searching for cool-looking seashells, and making castles from mounds of sand. Now in sandals and black tube socks tugged up high, pushing up our fogged-up bifocals from our sweaty noses, we tried not to twist our ankles as we maneuvered our way between blankets of women, as we were on full alert for topless women. We looked like a sad bunch, but alas we saw other groups of men doing the same thing so at least we were not alone. Exhausted after five minutes in the hot sun and trekking through the heavy sand, we headed back to the comforts of our lounge chairs by the pool.

Our wives, embracing some umbrella drinks, saw us and shook their heads in amazement, though after 15 or 20 years of marriage I'm not sure if any of us really amaze them anymore. We took off our shirts and nearly blinded some others lying around the pool with our bright white bodies that had been hibernating all winter up North. Most of us looked like we had not missed too many meals. Our wives were in no danger of us being swept away by some southern beauty. I'm not sure if they were happy or sad about that fact.

We submitted our pasty skin to two hours of the brutally hot sun, mocking the use of suntan lotion as something only kids need. We realized as we viewed our scorched backs in the bathroom mirror later and tried to walk on our nearly scarred ankles, that this was not a good conclusion.

We made reservations at one of the top steak restaurants in South Beach—a phenomenal place frequented by professional athletes, models, the "beautiful" people and visitors like us who have saved up all year for the chance to spend it in two hours. The place is so popular (even with reservations three months in advance) that we didn't get our order in until 11:00 p.m. which is about an hour after most of us are typically in dreamland in our own beds. We ordered giant steaks ranging from $50 to $88 after downing lots of $20 appetizers and $15 drinks, because that's what you are supposed to do at an expensive steak place. We got very nervous when we saw people with sad faces, shuffling slowly away from the ATM machine next door to the restaurant.

It was close to midnight when the main course finally arrived. We were already stuffed from the Kobe Beef slider appetizers, very tired and sunburned, but we tried to dive into the biggest piece of meat any of us had ever seen. We took a few bites and realized that we couldn't continue but then shoved in a few more bites to be sure. We barely noticed the piles and piles of creamed spinach, fried potatoes, asparagus and mushrooms we had also ordered, because that is also what you are supposed to do at an expensive steak place. The bill came and we were all stunned at the total amount and wondered if somehow we got the bill for the total restaurant. The waiter, whose children can afford to attend Harvard, Princeton and Stanford, was thrilled that his huge tip was automatically added on to the bill as he knew he would not have gotten that much money from us.

We asked for doggie bags and headed out with much lighter wallets. We were quickly followed by a conga line of stray dogs who looked particularly well-fed. We walked past one of the many happening Clubs for the beautiful people, well back behind the velvet ropes and soon realized that we had no chance of getting in. Young women with slinky dresses and giant breasts with no doggie bags seemed to be allowed in with ease.

We headed back to the hotel and looked for the refrigerator in our rooms, only to discover that none of our rooms had a refrigerator. We were not sure whether we'd risk food poisoning in the morning or just admit to our financial loss and stupid ordering.

When we tried to sleep later with three pounds of beef in our colon, no matter how fluffy the pillows were or how fresh the sheets were, we twisted and turned through the night with the smell of a rotting $88 porterhouse on the counter next to the TV.

We met up in the hotel bar for one last nightcap and arrived just before the bar was closing. We were all exhausted, so after one last drink we started to leave. As the first woman in our group made it to the door, some drunken guy started verbally abusing her with incredibly rude language for absolutely no reason, unless shots of tequilas and having your wife in another state count as good reasons.

We asked the guy to apologize and a near-fight ensued as the guy flew into an unexpected rage. The drunk (6'3" and 230 pounds) actually took off his shoes and started doing calisthenics in the bar (quite the site in a posh hotel bar) telling us he was warming up for a fight with us. Hotel security came over and watched this drunk rant and rave and threaten to beat us all up. (We didn't tell him we had so much food in us that we could barely move.) We assumed they were going to escort the drunk out, but then we learned that "membership does have its privileges."

The drunk pulled out his hotel Platinum card and demanded that *we* all get escorted out. The security guard then asked if any of us had Platinum hotel cards. We didn't. He informed us that Platinum members can pretty much do what they want and asked us to leave. We were stunned and showed three Elite cards and two Gold cards thinking our "full house" would beat his "one-of-a-kind," but we were sadly mistaken.

We reported the incident the next day to management. We think Mr. Platinum got upgraded to a suite once management became aware that he had an unpleasant evening threatening us.

When the next day was full of misadventures on the golf course and on the wave runners, we realized that the safest place was the hotel pool. For the next two days, we kept ourselves as hydrated as we could, at $10 a drink, and told funny stories that never seem to grow old. Who cares if the facts have changed so much over the years that no one knows where non-fiction ends and fiction begins?

I hope you have a set of friends like I do. And if you don't, we are available for a nominal fee—though none of us have Platinum cards.

Thar She Blows – Again and Again

We had numerous vodka parties in the driveways beginning at sundown, as no one wanted to be inside their dark houses. This also helped deaden the pain of being out thousands of dollars in repairs given high insurance deductibles.

The one place you definitely don't want to be in a hurricane is my house. Our 25-year-old wood-framed house would go down like the little pig's straw house from the Big Bad Wolf. We beg relatives, friends, neighbors with shutters, the mailman—anyone who might be willing to take my family in for a day or a week. They aren't usually willing to take us twice so we need a long list.

The South Florida Chamber of Commerce has these beautiful magazines and picturesque postcards of the stunningly attractive palm trees and sunsets. What they don't have is the devastation pictures from the massive hurricanes that hit South Florida the last few years. And the brochures don't tell you what people really do before, during and after a hurricane.

Hurricane season runs from June to November, though the bulk of the bad storms typically hit in August and September. You start to notice when the local news at 11:00 does not begin with a national murder investigation, a national missing person update or a story on Iraq, but with news of a drizzle in Africa (1500 miles and 2 weeks away) that could turn into the season's first big storm. Every day, people either rush home to see how the drizzle is directionally proceeding or surf a number of Internet sites to track the progress. Typically these drizzles turn out to be nothing, or they destroy whole island nations before they get to South Florida.

The year 2004 was no time for taking the storms lightly, as four giant storms hit "the Sunshine State." About five days before they hit land there is this giant cone of uncertainty visual that is shown around-the-clock on TV. The message is quite clear. Either stay where you are as there is a 50% chance you will get nailed, or if you decide to head out in any direction for lodging there is also a 50% chance you will get nailed. Plus there is a good chance if you try and outrun the storm by car, you will hit massive traffic jams where you will either run out of gas, have mechanical problems or have your kid's GameBoy batteries run out with no spares in the car.

There is also a black line in the middle of the "cone" that seems to pinpoint a particular house in a particular town, giving the absolute wrong impression that all other places will indeed be completely safe. Basically, the storms are so big and can change direction right up until the end. The safest thing is to get prepared several days in advance and batten down the hatches with plywood, aluminum shutters and have plenty of batteries, canned food and water on hand. Or if you can, take a plane trip to Nebraska. In my house, my shikshe (non-Jewish) wife is responsible for all of the manual labor while I am in charge of watching the cone of uncertainty on TV, not necessarily fair but someone like me who excels at TV really needs to be at the helm of the remote control.

In the end, the meteorologists provide very little helpful information since they just don't know which way storms will "wobble" (the technical term for "Oh Shoot—it's now coming my way") at the end. By the fourth day of being awake virtually 20 hours a day, they look so punchy they barely appear credible at that point. Worse than the "inside reporters" are the crazy ones who stand on the breaking-apart, ocean fishing piers in the middle of the storm battered by storm surge and rain, trying to scream into their microphones above the roar of the waves, telling the viewers (many of whom have already lost power and can't see them anyway) that it is raining pretty hard. "Oh, really," we all think from our shuttered-in homes. Sometimes they instead stand in the middle of retail store parking lots dodging giant metal signs that are being flung around by the 100 mph winds.

For the first and most severe of the 2004 hurricanes, my brother and his new wife (surprisingly still married after a week of my family living with them) allowed us to stay with them in their concrete house fortified with strong metal shutters. We had planned on just showing up and hanging out, but almost as soon as we arrived there was lots of work to be done. Putting up the heavy shutters was a major pain, putting batteries in 12 flashlights and six radios seemed like overkill, and making 24 peanut butter and jelly sandwiches in advance seemed unsavory. We also had to siphon the swimming pool so it wouldn't start overflowing once the heavy rains came.

Since I was in charge of tuning the radios to the sports call-in radio station (how many stories of safety precautions can you listen to), my wife took on the task of siphoning a foot of water out of my brother's pool with this giant hose. She was extremely good at it but was exhausted after 30 minutes. Barely having caught her breath, she saw how much trouble my brother's 85-year-old neighbor (Irving) was having trying to use buckets to get water out of his pool. She said in slow, deep, tired breaths, "Would__you___ like___ me_ __ to___ suck___ your___ hose?" The smile on that guy's face was something I will never forget. Beat red, he said he unfortunately had to worry about the hurricane right now but he would be available on Saturday if the offer were still good. My wife stayed indoors, and away from Irving, for the next five days straight.

That night the wind howled and we got little sleep. It turns out if you don't screw in the shutters just right (I must admit I somehow screwed up screwing), the noise sounds like you are stuck in a subway station with trains rushing by.

We lost power around 8:00 p.m. so there was no TV and no electricity. Sitting for hours in candlelight reminiscing about the good old days of air-conditioning was a lot of fun for about 15 minutes, but grew older and older as five days passed. With no TV distraction, it also gave our family a great opportunity to spend quality time discussing our dreams and lives. We did that for five minutes the first night and decided that playing Uno by candlelight was far less stressful.

On day six, we were finally able to go home, only to be greeted by a 50-foot tree that had crashed into our driveway, narrowly missing our garage and roof. It took six hours of sawing, chopping, and carrying branches in extreme humidity to get it out of the driveway. I felt so bad for my wife, who did that job. I was in charge of staying near the TV in case the power got restored.

We actually got to meet many of our neighbors who are usually holed up in their houses busily sawing giant limbs or removing shutters from their windows after the storm. We had numerous vodka parties in the driveways beginning at sundown, as no one wanted to be inside their dark houses. This also helped deaden the pain of being out thousands of dollars in repairs given high insurance deductibles. It was kind of weird being buzzed watching the neighborhood kids climb broken trees and see if they would land safely as half-torn off branches fell to the ground from their weight. The smaller kids served as testers.

I finally got to go to work the next day, and was greeted by no traffic lights working and no cops directing traffic. With Boca normally being a bad place to drive, it didn't help having tired, angry, smelly, cabin-fever, tuna-eating people negotiating to see who would crash through the intersections first. It was like playing demolition derby after a week of not sleeping. There were some really cool-looking fender benders though.

With my office being 35 miles south of Boca and away from the brunt of the storm, it was so nice to feel the coolness of air-conditioning (my partner caught me sniffing the air vents, which I guess did not look that professional though I didn't really care). I also felt very powerful clicking on a light switch and actually having it do something.

People freak out every hurricane season and absolute hate its arrival. The only person who seems to look forward to the season every year is now 87-year-old Irving who every August calls my wife asking pleadingly if the "deal is still on."

Behind the Wheel

Like ants descending on a piece of rotting fruit, the elevators in places like Century Village (a very large retirement community) start humming, community busses start revving their engines, and people storm out of their apartments and homes (so quickly by foot it does make you wonder how each one seems to have a handicap sticker) to get to the restaurants that offer $2-$3 off the meal if you're seated hours before others would normally go out to a restaurant.

I've been told I'm one of the worst drivers people have ever come across, and that's from my family and friends. On the road, I often get the one-finger salutes from fellow drivers who until recently I thought were simply waving to me. I have never received a ticket in over 30 years of driving and never hit anyone. The two biggest complaints are that I drive the speed limit and that I begin signaling that I am getting off a highway exit about one mile from the ramp. Now those don't seem like big crimes or reasons for these accusations and "finger-pointing."

Now I must admit I did fail my driver's test twice when I was in my late teens. The first failure was when I was making a right hand turn (the final turn into the driver's ed lot) whereby I somehow managed to drive over the curb with both my front and back tires and almost made the car go perpendicular to the road like some stunt driver going through a narrow alley. While my instructor almost had a heart attack to go along with his bruised ribs, the other students waiting to follow me who saw the whole event were either really confident that they couldn't repeat that or scared that maybe one's nerves could get the best of them.

My car finally flattened out and there were actually four tires on the pavement, and I was able to come to a complete stop. The instructor looked at me with the widest eyes I have seen to this day, especially when I asked him if I passed (since I didn't screw up until the end) or if I could repeat that last part of the driving test right then. He pulled out his pen and was about to write the biggest X he had ever written, when it became apparent his pen had snapped in two and ink was all over his clothes and the car.

My second failure three weeks later was more related to nicking a lady's dog who seemed to come out from nowhere as I was carefully making sure I didn't hit any curbs like I did on my first go-around. I was fairly certain that the dog only had a minor limp, but the vet assured me in the settlement phase that it was a "pronounced, permanent limp."

After living in South Florida for the last 25 years, I have developed a few theories on why driving down here is so bad.

First of all, so few of the drivers are born and raised Floridians. Tons of New Yorkers, tons of Latin Americans, tons of tourists, tons of people who just relocated here, tons of "snowbirds" who only come down for a few months out of the year, etc. All of these people are used to their own rules of the road from wherever they came, and many are not all that familiar with where they are even supposed to be going. It's especially bad when you get lost in certain places in Miami where English is barely spoken. From my fifth-grade Spanish class I have been known to try the two phrases that still are stuck in my sub-conscious: "Dónde está el baño?" (Where is the bathroom?) and "Mi libro es rojo." (My book is red). I have found that neither of these has been particularly helpful in getting to my planned destination.

Second, the age of the driving population is about as wide as you would see probably anywhere in the world. Kids can get their learner's permit at age 15 and their full license at age 16. I hadn't even failed my two tests by that age. Some are so short at that age it's hard to tell if they can even see the road while they're driving. Plus, they often drive like one of their car racing video games. At the other end of the spectrum are the retirees who are often driving into their 90's. While there are so many cars with handicapped stickers, I must admit I did get nervous driving behind one guy who had a sticker on his car that said "Partially Blind."

Third, is the phenomenal number of these diverse groups all seemingly on the road at exactly 5:00 p.m. Besides the typical rush-hour traffic in all metro areas, we have a unique mad-rush called the "Early Bird Dinner" attack. Like ants descending on a piece of rotting fruit, the elevators in places like Century Village (a very large retirement community) start humming, community busses start revving their engines, and people storm out of their apartments and homes (so quickly by foot it does make you wonder how each one seems to have a handicap sticker) to get to the restaurants that offer $2-$3 off the meal if you're seated before others would normally go out to a restaurant. The roads are insane, the parking lots are insane and the restaurants are insane. At least people get to save some bucks, though I do hear people then whine "Murray, it's only 5:20 now—what are we going to do for the rest of the night?"

Fourth is the extreme weather. It can be a beautiful day, with convertible tops rolled down and out of nowhere a torrential rain will start pummeling the roads. It's tricky either driving a convertible trying to get its top up at 60 mph or driving behind a couple of those. Plus it gets so hot in the summer time, popping into a car in the middle of the day is liking sticking your head in a microwave. I've seen people who actually use pot holders to buckle their seat belt and hold onto the steering wheel. Now that makes for some interesting turning.

Finally, I believe that Jewish people are at a biological and ethnic disadvantage in general when it comes to driving. Given the large population of Jewish people in South Florida, I think that also explains part of the problem driving down here.

When one thinks of great drivers, names like Mario Andretti, Emerson Fittapaldi, and Dale Earnhardt come to mind. You rarely hear how Saul Horowitz maneuvered his way through the traffic at the Daytona 500 to narrowly beat out Bernie Cohen.

Most of the Jews in Florida, just like me, grew up in New York. We were trained on the subway system, busses, hailing cabs and walking to get to places. I barely remember my parents even having a car. Once a month we would dust it off to go visit my grandmother in the Bronx until the tires were stolen on one trip. So how can one reasonably expect Jewish New Yorkers to arrive in Florida for three or four months out of the year, rent a car and be good drivers—especially since most of the time they are all-charged up trying to beat the crowd to the Early Bird dinner?

The bottom line is that when I hear that I'm such a bad driver, I turn to the people huddled in the back seat of my car surrounded by protective covering and point out that it's not completely my fault. One advantage is that when we go out on dates with other couples, no one ever asks me to drive. I remember even offering to be a designated driver one New Year's Eve and one drunken friend of mine slurred something like, "I'd have a better chance of making it home with five drinks in me, than with you driving me home straight."

Summertime at the Ballpark

I was stunned at just how much crappy food three boys and I could consume in two hours. There's nothing quite like taking your son to a major league baseball game. As I found out, there's really nothing quite like taking your 10-year old son and two of his friends (Matthew and Korey) to a major league game.

The Friday night game was a showdown between two teams (Marlins and Phillies) tied for the Wild Card playoff hunt with only 15 games left in the season. Every pitch, every batter and every inning was important—at least to the Marlins, Phillies, me, and most of the 40,000 people at the game.

The cost to get into the game was insane and became increasingly worse when I started to feed the boys with their insatiable appetites. Box seats were $35 apiece, so for $140 for the four tickets, plus $10 for parking and gas/tolls of another $10, we were in our seats for $160.

We had good seats, about 20 rows behind home plate right in the *middle* of a row of 32 people. The temperature at the start of the game was 90 degrees and the only breeze I felt was from the 285-pound guy squeezed next to me who was ripping off hot dog wrappers at a furious rate.

We had gotten to the game early as I didn't want to battle the traffic driving to the game, deal with the parking lot nightmare, or fight the crowds getting to their seats. As we got to our seats, the boys entered into furious games on their Nintendo GameBoys. I tried to explain to them the history of baseball, the excitement of the pennant race and the subtleties of what to look out for in tonight's game. They looked at me blankly and quickly got their fingers cranking on their electronic umbilical cord.

Since we were about 45 minutes early and the stadium was relatively empty, I asked if they were hungry or had to go to the bathroom. Without lifting their heads, I got three grunts that I interpreted as, "We're on one of the hardest levels imaginable in the video game, so do not interrupt us." I sat back and watched batting practice as players bashed home runs, checked out the ever-changing scoreboard to keep up with the latest changes in the standings, and listened to the great sounds of "Peanuts, get your peanuts" or "Beer here, ice-cold beer here." I'm a sports addict, so I was in heaven.

Finally the crowds started piling in and our row filled up with people of all ages and sizes, though none appeared to have ever completed a Weight Watchers class. The game got underway and the Marlins took a quick 2-0 lead in the first inning on a long home run by their clean-up hitter. The crowd was on its feet screaming wildly.

The Phillies loaded the bases in the top of the second with one out when one of my son's friends announced that he "really, really had to go the bathroom." Fifteen minutes before, when it was easy to get to the aisle from our middle seats, it hadn't been a thought in his brain. We waited until the 285-pound guy had swallowed his fifth hotdog of the night and headed in that direction. Some people stood, some scrunched their knees, and some made us hop over them. Many of them were clearly not happy. We made it to the aisle and quickly hurried to the bathroom. He was doing his thing when we heard a tremendous roar. The Marlins had just pulled off a spectacular double play. We got back to the aisle as people were raving about how great a play they just witnessed. At the time of the great play, I was watching 19 empty urinals lined up with "my"10-year-old kid using the 20th.

Again knocking into people as we made it back to the middle of the row, the 10-year-old committed a cardinal sin, perhaps the all-time cardinal sin at a baseball game. He bumped into a guy's beer and it spilled all over the guy's lap. This guy was about 65 years old and looked liked he had just left the Giorgio Armani shop on South Beach, a fancy men's hair salon or a plastic surgeon's office. His date was a 25-year-old blonde with fake boobs that she kept on propping up throughout the game trying to get people to notice her. I was eight seats down and I must admit I did catch a glimpse of her once or twice before the incident. Neither was particularly lenient on the 10-year-old or me as they came out with four-letter words I had rarely heard before. I gave the girlfriend a whole bunch of napkins and watched as she vigorously tried to dry her boyfriend off. While I thought it was just our row watching this, it was quite hilarious to see this broadcast on the JumboTron.

The camera guy certainly had a great sense of humor and timing. Now 40,000 people had a golden opportunity to view the show. In hindsight, it was a heck of a beer bump.

After about 10 minutes in our seats with the people in our row relatively calmed down, my son announced that he was absolutely starving. We waited 20 minutes for a vendor to appear but all we saw were guys pushing beer. We decided to walk the other way down our row and had similar bumping experiences, though fortunately no beer was spilled. We got some peanuts, pretzels, popcorn, ice cream and soda for all of us (quite the healthy treats) all for the low, low price of about $65. We didn't miss any great plays while we were gone and got back to our seats without much hassle.

Over the next three innings the other boy had to go the bathroom, and another after eating a bag of salty pretzels needed me to get him some water. I believe we were the most hated row-mates in the stadium as I continued to get up and accompany whichever boy needed to go somewhere or get something. I wasn't even sure who was winning or what was going on the field as I was too tired from banging into people and leaving our seats so regularly.

I told them in the sixth inning that I was making one last trip out of our seats no matter what. One of the boys came with me to go the bathroom as the other two continued to shove cotton candy into their mouths that I just bought from another "healthy vendor." I was stunned at just how much crappy food three boys and I could consume in two hours. I'm sure their mothers wouldn't have approved, but I guess that's part of being a father.

I went to an open urinal and as I was doing my thing I heard, "Arnie Goldberg, is that you?" I have never been sure about stadium urinal etiquette. Do you wait until you're done to respond, do you immediately turn your head and look the person in the eyes, do you instead look down to see if they're done peeing? I turned my head and saw a person (who had just finished peeing) who I hadn't seen in about 10 years. He was so thrilled to see me that he stuck out his hand to shake hands. While I didn't want to be rude to a long-ago friend, my hands were occupied, plus I knew where his hand had just been, so I kind of nodded hello (maybe that's why the Japanese bow). We agreed to meet outside the bathroom. We talked for about 10 minutes. I felt a little embarrassed when after seeing my t-shirt with ice cream stains, and cotton candy schmush (not sure if that's a real word, but that's what was on my shirt) and my two-week-old beard, he asked, "You're not working, are you?" I then remembered we were missing the game and I had left two 10-year-olds by themselves for too long. Another typical fatherhood moment.

As I rushed back, the usher stopped me at the top of the tunnel leading to the seats, saying that I wasn't allowed to go to my seats while a player was batting, as it was obnoxious to others. I didn't think my group could be any more obnoxious than we had already been, so I pleaded with the guy to let me sit down. He refused and I got a little madder. While we were arguing, a screaming foul ball came flying about 15 feet over my head into the front row of the deck overhead. I could hear the crunching of fingers, and saw three guys jumping on top of the guy with the seemingly broken hand fighting for the ball. As I started turning my back to argue with the usher some more, I saw one of the prettiest sites I have ever seen at a ballgame: a major league baseball was falling gently from 10 feet above me and heading right towards me in what seemed like slow motion. I stuck out my hands in disbelief, dodging the blood droplets from the deck above, and caught the feather-like weighted ball. It was the first time I had ever even come close to catching a ball and I never dreamed it would be so painless.

A guy rushed over to me and offered me $5 for the ball, which I politely refused. He then offered $10 which I refused again. He then told me he would make me his final offer of $15. I told him I had spent $160 to get to the game and another $70 on food and drinks. His $15 wasn't going to offset the costs, plus it was a dream to actually catch a ball. I wasn't going to just give it away.

As the Phillies started pounding out hit after hit and the Marlins' errors got more and more embarrassing, it was time to head home to beat the crowd. We knocked into people for the last time, and I apologized to the guy with the wet lap and his girlfriend, who seemed relieved we were leaving.

We left the stadium at 10:00 p.m. The kids were absolutely wired from all their sugar consumption and became quite difficult to control in the craziness of the parking lot as I tried to remember where the heck I had parked. After 30 minutes of walking up and down numerous aisles, I found my car only about 10 feet from where I had first started looking.

I was hoping the boys would be tired at this time of night, but the sugar and their GameBoys kept them buzzed for the

45-minute drive home. Ten minutes from home one of the boys complained that his stomach was killing him and that he needed to "barf." Lovely, I thought. I asked if he could make it to his own house to do this but he said no, so I had to pull over and watch the kid heave up about $25 of food (I use this term loosely) that I had bought him.

We finally made it home and my wife asked me how the game was. I thought about how I missed most of the game "running errands," how the Marlins had gotten crushed in an important game, about the guy with the wet groin we had caused, how I couldn't find my car, about my son's friend vomiting, and the $230 I was out. I simply smiled and said, "I caught my first baseball."

6. Looking Back, Giving Back, and Going Back

A S MY FAVORITE ESPN Sportscaster likes to say, "Back, Back, Back, Back . . ." It is great to reflect back on funny experiences at work, at school and in trying to help others.

Boss: A Four-Letter Word?

Arnie, we're glad you are on board, but I have one request for you. I need you to be a woman. Now all kinds of things started racing through my mind.

Most people work in their life for over 40 years, and that's not even counting part-time jobs before the "real" working world.

In looking back over the many years I've worked, it's interesting to think back to the five companies I worked for and 13 (an unlucky number?) different bosses I've had. Now I'm not sure if I've had the average experience or not, but either I attract some bizarre bosses (very possible) or there are just so many weird people out there in leadership roles that the law of averages caught up with me. It's probably a bit of both.

I've worked in the insanely snowy cold of Syracuse, in the unbelievably crowded but thrilling Tokyo, in the heat of South Florida, and in beautiful (yes, really) Montclair, New Jersey. I have worked for giant companies like GE and Motorola and helped create three Internet start-ups during both the rise and collapse of Internet businesses. All along the way, I never really knew who my next boss would be or even what my next job would be. The one constant was that I had some "interesting" bosses.

I've had straight-laced bosses who were so uptight I thought their heads would eventually explode. On the opposite end, I've had hard-core partying bosses whose synapses have probably melted along the way. It was tough keeping up with those guys but I sure tried hard.

When I worked in Japan, my boss spoke about three words of English. I never had a clue in three years if what I was doing for him was what he wanted. The good news is that he liked to drink lots of sake every night, so the international language of red-faced, drunkenness seemed to provide a great common bond. Thank goodness I knew the word *sayonara,* or he may still have expected me on Monday morning —15 years ago.

I had a bi-polar boss who was ridiculously happy one day (or part of a day) and unbelievably catastrophic another day. I felt that I was experiencing constant whiplash. One day he would walk in and say that he was up all last night convinced that all our clients were going to cancel contracts that very day—just a premonition. If we got a new client, he would rejoice like he had won the Powerball lottery. He was continuously surprised when no one would ride along with him to the abyss on those "dark" days or soar along up into the sky if we got a new client. We all called him "Jack" as in "Hi-Low" and took bets throughout the week as to the roller coaster positions on certain days.

I've had bosses that were put in charge above me and my division after they got booted out of very senior jobs due to sexual harassment or mental instability, and they needed to be hidden away for a couple of years. Hidden from everyone except for my troops and me, that is!

One of my most interesting bosses was a phenomenal author who had the vision of trying to create an iPod/iTunes-like Internet business 10 years before iPod came to be and five years before downloading of audio/music even became remotely popular. It was in the early days of the Internet before Netscape went public, before Amazon, etc. I thought it was a great opportunity to get in on the ground floor of something new and exciting and away from my boss still stuck in the penalty box—above me. It was a great two years but in the early days of the Internet, money started drying up and creating new businesses out of thin air was much harder than the business plans projected. That being said, about 80% of the employees, including me, were downsized one day. Most of them were simply called into their boss's office on Friday and told the bad news. Since Don had personally hired me, he came over to my house to deliver the news. He asked that we take a walk around the block. Now my NJ neighborhood had some long blocks and it was about 20 degrees and blowing when we started our walk. While it's not great being fired, it certainly sucks worse being a half mile from your house with the guy that just fired you in the freezing cold, since there just isn't much to say and there still is quite a bit of distance to go.

My favorite boss was Frank who I worked for during a two-year period at Motorola. He was brilliant about technology and business, but knew more about the Grateful Dead than a person making more than $200K per year would ever admit. He was a very senior guy and wore his tie-dye shirts, with his scraggly beard and long hair to every meeting. He delivered results and he didn't care. His people would run through walls for him.

We traveled internationally quite a bit together in the late 80's to little villages in China, out-of-the-way cities in Russia and bizarre locations in South America. Thrilling for sure, and we never really felt unsafe until we got the call from headquarters' Security Intelligence in Chicago to come immediately to be debriefed before our first trip to Russia. Three former CIA types sat us down (not a smile among them) and launched into this speech that they've heard the two of us tend to live on the wild side, but upon entering Russian airspace we should go into complete serious mode for the duration of the trip. We were both a little surprised at their intensity and I decided I would follow their lead. Not Frank. We were about to land in Moscow and I saw that my carry-on bag was filled with all kinds of anti-Soviet propaganda that Frank stuffed in there while I was asleep. I started sweating like the guy from *Midnight Express* with the hashish attached to his body. I made my way to the bathroom (I definitely needed it) and proceeded to dump the stuff in the disposal. I never saw anyone laugh so hard in my life when I got back to my seat.

After recovering from that, our local Russian contact decided to take us to the exhibition hockey match between the Russian Elite Army Hockey team and the NHL Atlanta

Flames. Let's just say that of the 18,000 people in the stands there weren't too many pulling for the Flames. After about five shots of vodka, and an equal number of beers, Frank tells me it's "customary" to start the "wave" when Atlanta was doing something well. High on alcohol, tired from the jet lag, or still stunned from the disposal of the spy books, I started right in with him. It's definitely weird to do a two-man wave with thousands of people looking at you like you just got off a plane from Boca Raton. But to Frank's credit, the Russian fans were at least as equally toasted as we were and a few of them joined in with the wave. Amazingly, just a few minutes later there were hundreds doing it and by the end of the game, almost the whole stadium was. It was one of the more spectacular things I've ever seen. We did not report this back to Security.

When I think back to perhaps the most unusual boss, I've got to think of the weight loss company I worked for about 15 years ago. I was hired to be in their customer service department answering emails, primarily from women struggling with their weight. On the very first day, after spending five hours in a general orientation program about the company, I was asked to meet privately with the boss.

"Arnie, we're glad you are on board, but I have one request for you. I need you to be a woman." Now all kinds of things started racing through my mind. I had just quit a decent job to join this company and I had no idea what was being asked of me. I stammered something like, "You want me to wear a dress?"

He laughed and said "No, I just need you to act like a woman when you are doing email customer service, as 85% of our members are women and they like talking to other women about their weight struggles. I was thinking that it makes sense to keep your initials of A.G., so how about Angela Goldberg or Alice Goldberg."

I had never had to make a name decision like that before and couldn't really figure out the key variables in why Angela might be better than Alice, but somewhere in the back of my mind was that Jefferson Airplane *White Rabbit* song lyric, "Go ask Alice, I think she'll know." So on that day I became Alice Goldberg. I did not rush out to tell my parents that they now had that daughter they had long ago wished for.

Email is scary, as you can really be anyone. From that first day on, I was Alice Goldberg to hundreds and hundreds of women trying to shed those last 15 or 100 pounds. At first it was pretty easy. I just answered basic questions about nutrition and fitness and simply finished my email with "Best of health, Alice." Then it got progressively more difficult and weirder as I had to learn way more than any man should about things like PMS, breastfeeding, and sports bras.

Problems began to surface a few weeks later, as many of these women wanted to bond with me and starting asking me more personal questions. They were starting off their emails with, "Hey, girlfriend," They wanted to know about my love life, what movies I saw recently, and what I thought about the latest issue of *Cosmo*.

I then entered full actor mode, or was it actress mode? I started subscribing to *Cosmo*, *Glamour* and *Style*. I went to chick flicks and took cooking lessons. My wife was beyond concerned since I hadn't told her the whole Alice story yet. In fact, I was too embarrassed to tell her even *part* of the Alice story. She thought she was losing me. I was just trying to be the best woman I knew how to be.

After six months, I couldn't take it any longer and had to quit. I felt bad, as my boss said I was the best "girl" he had. Even now, it's weird for me, when at a party, I hear one woman yell out to another, "Hey, girlfriend." I automatically turn in that direction to see if someone is trying to get my attention.

To all of my bosses, I must admit I learned a lot of things to both do and not do from you. Hopefully in my many years of leading people, I have done mostly the right things. To all of you who have had similar bosses, I hope you enjoyed the experiences, and to all of you who are bosses now—lighten up and enjoy!

Hangin' with the Homeless

A few people did complain that the beef was cold or that the bread was stale or that the beans were watery. It reminded me of a typical listening experience in a Boca Raton diner.

There's nothing funny about being homeless, so I'm not sure how humor and the homeless intersected for me. I've seen the homeless on the side of the road, I've seen the homeless on street corners and medians begging for money, and I've seen documentaries on the plight of the homeless. I've always felt a "rolled up car window" away from the homeless.

My in-laws do volunteer work at a Soup Kitchen (Faith Café) in Tampa every Monday for lunch and have for years. Assuming there is a Heaven, my in-laws will be seated in the first row with top accommodations. I may be in the balcony with some stale peanuts to munch on. While visiting there on vacation, they asked if my wife, two boys and I would like to help out the next day. My first three initial silent reactions were "No," "No," and "No," as I selfishly wanted to do some sight-seeing and wasn't thrilled with being around 100 unbathed, potentially deranged people. My wife reminded me to think of it as return to my college-like experience for two hours. With that persuasive thought in mind, I agreed. I had no idea what to expect.

We arrived at the Faith Café around 11:00 on the morning of July 4th to help set up. It was about 92 degrees outside, though nice and air-conditioned inside. My boys and I put out the napkins, plastic utensils and drink cups, while about 10 other volunteers prepared the barbecued beef, corn, beans, corn bread and desserts.

At 11:30 sharp, the doors opened and about 75 sweaty people shuffled in. Many of them had ridden their rickety bikes to the Café from many miles away in the blistering heat. They looked to be in better physical shape than I was, which my boys pointed out to me. Honesty only goes so far I reminded them. My boys and I still had "front room" duty and proceeded to hand each one a full plate of food as they sat down. We were not to be confused with having any type of waiter experience, but we only spilled a little and did not put our hands into too many of the plates before serving them.

The homeless were incredibly polite and thankful, much more so than the people I typically run across. There were definitely a few that were "out of it" but they thought the beef was delicious so there was some upside. It was a bit surprising to see how many looked and sounded like "normal" people—well, at least normal people that I know.

All was going well until a couple of the homeless men meandered over to me, and seeing my stained tee-shirt, torn shorts, and straggly beard (I wasn't sure what to wear to a Soup Kitchen) they asked if I slept under the bridge or downtown. I hate to admit it but they were two of the more coherent and observant of the bunch. Before I could get the stunned look off my face, they casually mentioned that if I happened to be sleeping under the bridge tonight, around 9:00 there would be a good view of the fireworks show. I pulled out my electronic organizer and took that note.

Then an old woman carrying all of her possessions in a ratty knapsack said through her four remaining teeth, "Sonny, you look new to the streets but I do recommend the public bath place down the road since you could use it." I was flabbergasted, even though my wife had said the same thing in the car on the way over.

As the people began to ask for seconds and thirds (they looked like me eating while breaking a Yom Kippur fast) I began to warm up to the more chatty ones. One was a baseball fanatic who knew more stats than I did, which is saying a lot, and loved the Red Sox as evidenced by his tattered cap. We were actually high-fiving about beating the Yankees down three games to zero in the American League Championship series. Another was a movie trivia buff who knew all kinds of details about both past and current movies. I couldn't imagine him going to Muvico regularly, owning a satellite dish, or being a NetFlix subscriber, so I wasn't quite sure how he knew so much.

A few people did complain that the beef was cold or that

the bread was stale or that the beans were watery. It reminded me of a typical listening experience in a Boca Raton diner.

Speaking of Boca, I'm back home now and volunteering in a local soup kitchen feeding the homeless. I actually bathe more frequently but the guests still look at me like I might be one of them.

30-Year
High School Reunion

*While we knew that giving away free ice cream was bad
for the owner's business, it really was a matter of our
survival in the high school jungle.*

I graduated from JFK High School in Plainview, Long
Island, in the mid-70's along with several hundred others.

While there's nothing like hanging out on the couch in
the summertime in Florida and relaxing, I was intrigued by
a potential trip to Long Island for my 30-year high school
reunion. I decided to take the plunge and tie in some family
time while I was up there.

I was surprised how many people actually showed up at
the reunion. I'm pretty sure that most high schools back then
and probably still today, had their cliques or groups. Ours
certainly did. The groups I remember (with some overlap)
were:

Brainiacs—eyeglasses, always studying, in Advanced Placement classes since kindergarten, not at a lot of parties.

'Hoods (as in hoodlums)—stole people's lunches and lunch money, had beards at age 14, were left back at least once or twice, drove cars with no mufflers, smoked cigarettes a lot.

Preppies—above–average smart, above-average wealthy, lots of clique parties, dressed in latest fashions.

Druggies—long hair, dirty, happy and/or zombie like, rarely in class.

Ghosts—pictured in yearbook but no one can recall having ever seen these people. Not sure if filler for yearbook or just people who could make themselves invisible.

Jocks—athletic, loud, strong, popular, egotistical.

Sluts—trashy looking, some popular, some popular for only one reason.

Nerds—weird-looking, above-average smart, skinny from getting lunch money stolen daily by 'hoods or jocks.

It was clear who was in which group during lunchtime when the various groups went to their spots in the cafeteria— except for the Ghosts.

When I think back, I actually was in my own group with my best friend, Mike Greenberg. We were smart, but not quite in the brainiac group since we liked to have fun. We weren't preppies since we found them to be relatively "plastic," and no one back then or now would ever mistake me for being into the latest fashion. As for the rest of the groups, we just didn't fit in.

That's not to say we didn't try to be friends with some of the people in some of the groups. In fact, our first logical target was the Sluts, but they just wanted to be friends, which was disheartening since they were sleeping with most everyone else.

Going to the cafeteria was quite the challenge for Mike and me. While many people were friendly to us in our classes and in the hallways, when it came to the cafeteria we just weren't welcome in "their" spot. It was kind of strange looking for a table for two when all the cafeteria tables were these gigantic rectangle tables.

After months and months of this, we stumbled onto a lucky break. Mike and another friend of mine (Andy) had gotten a job at the main ice cream store in town where everyone went. I hung out there on weekends pitching in for free ice cream.

First the Druggies would come on Friday nights, stoned out of their minds with uncontrollable munchies. Mike or I would give them either some free ice cream or some extra toppings that absolutely delighted them.

The Brainiacs and Preppies would come next as they returned from the library, and we would do the same. The Jocks would show up right before closing time, pretty drunk, and they would be well-cared for as well. The Sluts came, often with the 'Hoods after the doors were locked, but we quickly learned that it was better to re-open for them than to have your car tires flattened by accident. The Nerds did not show up, nor the Ghosts.

By the time that first weekend was over, we were like

celebrities in town (though the Druggies forgot they had been to the ice cream store). Mike and I still had no group, but on that first Monday we were welcomed to sit on the outskirts of each of the group's main areas in the cafeteria. What an accomplishment!

While we knew that giving away free ice cream was bad for the owner's business, it really was a matter of our survival in the high school jungle. We felt bad when the business collapsed, but got over our misery when the Sluts started hanging out with us more and more.

Mike and I have stayed in limited contact over the last 30 years as we went off in different directions, with Mike based in Oakland/San Fran and me based in Florida. As the 30-year reunion approached we got in touch and decided to go. We were curious to see how much people had changed.

It was great catching up with Mike on the phone and via email before the reunion. Even after so many years, the reason we were such good friends came flowing back and our conversations flowed easily as though no time had passed.

We showed up together at the reunion along with about 150 others, a pretty sizeable turnout after all those years. The Ghosts did not attend and some of the 'Hoods were either in jail or wearing electronic bracelets and could not leave their jurisdiction. But for the most part, the other groups did show up. It was funny to see them assemble in the giant ballroom in almost the exact same way they did in the cafeteria 30 years before.

As expected, the Brainiacs went on to Harvard and Princeton and became doctors, lawyers and leaders in their communities. The Preppies went on to decent colleges and became businessmen and chiropractors. The Druggies went in two different directions. They had either continued on in their ways and looked about 70 years old, or had been through rehab and were nervous about drinking soda due to the caffeine.

The Jocks for the most part had not aged particularly gracefully. Plus, while they were the heroes in high school, most of them were not the athletic greats in college and certainly not beyond, which left them with some dented egos. The Nerds had become engineers and accountants. The Sluts had become grade school teachers.

Mike (who is a very successful lawyer and graduate of Stanford) and I (along with Andy, Rusty, Gregg and a few others) sat at our own table most of the night reminiscing, and periodically we were joined by some others from different groups. It was a fun night that went by too quickly.

After the main course was served, it was nice to see the standing ovation Mike got when he took over the ice cream station.

Postscript

I started off this comedy book with a story about a hospice, odd to say the least. It seems equally strange to finish the book by talking about cancer—another less-than-happy topic.

When I had written only a few chapters, one of my son's favorite teachers and someone I had come to know through various school events, was diagnosed with cancer. Barbara is someone who loves to laugh and loves to help children learn and develop. Obviously she was devastated. Once she had begun treatment, I decided to send her one chapter to try and cheer her up even for a few minutes. She loved the chapter I sent and asked for me to send some more weekly.

Since I only had a few written, she had pretty much tapped me out quickly and she still had a long way to go in her treatment. I committed myself to writing a chapter every week—not an easy task if you've ever tried writing a book while juggling a full-time job and a full-time life with a wife and two young boys.

By waking up early in the mornings or writing once everyone had gone to bed, I stuck to my commitment and sent a chapter to Barbara every week. She said she would laugh hysterically reading them over and over again, and always looked forward to the next chapter.

By the time I had sent the last one, six months had passed since she had begun treatment. She was feeling much better, and fortunately the cancer was in remission and has been for over a year now.

They say laughter is the best medicine. While it doesn't cure cancer, Barbara told me that it kept her spirits higher and that she was able to fight just a little bit harder.

Knowing that someone could feel better through some of my craziness captured in print made me feel great!

As I have now started to promote the book, every day I wake up hoping that I can make at least one person laugh out loud. And I hope they feel like doing the same for someone they know.

If you know someone who loves to laugh or could use a laugh, several chapters of this book are on the website (www. whyjewsdontcamp.com) for free (both Jews and non-Jews love free stuff you know!) to email your friends, relatives, etc. You can also order the book on the website, from Amazon. com or find it at your local bookstore.

Who do you know that would laugh the most from this book?

- Best friend/other friends	- Boss/Colleague at work
- Spouse	- Teacher
- Mom or Dad	- Son or Daughter
- Brother or Sister	- Relative
- Book club member	

Portions of the proceeds of the sale of this book will go the American Cancer Society, the National Jewish Federation, and the Palm Beach Hospice.

Thanks for reading this book and I really hope you enjoyed it. I'd love to hear from you, so feel free to email your thoughts, jokes, or comments to arnie@whyjewsdontcamp.com. I'm also available for speaking engagements as well.

About
Laugh Out Loud Publishing

Laugh Out Loud (LOL) Publishing (www.LOLpub.com) began as a response to very funny writers being rejected by the large publishing houses. Fresh, hilarious authors are rejected because they are simply not famous and thus harder to promote. LOL Publishing believes that great humor should not be that easily discarded.

The company is dedicated to:

1) Making people laugh via the written or spoken word.

2) Helping others make people laugh by facilitating them in getting their work out into the marketplace.

3) Donating a portion of the company's sales to charitable organizations.

Consumers: LOL Publishing relies on creative, irreverent marketing and a great Internet viral community to get the word about their authors and their really funny work. Please help us spread the word! Dig into your email contact list and email some free chapters from our authors! Visit www. whyjewsdontcamp.com and www.LOLpub.com for the free chapters.

Prospective Authors: Send us an email to discuss your work to Steve@LOLpub.com. And if you want send us a copy of your most bizarre rejection letters. We've got quite the collection that is truly hard to believe!